KU-688-144

JASPER'S TREASURE

In Stellenbosch, in the wine growing area of South Africa, Lexi owns a teashop. Her grandparents rent a farm, Sunnyfields, growing berries, and Lexi sells the jams they produce. It's a good life. Then Lexi meets Jasper Rousseau and she's attracted to him. But Jasper, who's inherited a wine estate, has a scheming brother. When Roger jeopardises Lexi and her grandparents' lives and ruins all their years of hard work, can Lexi learn to trust Jasper again?

Books by Beverley Winter
in the Linford Romance Library:

HOUSE ON THE HILL
A TIME TO LOVE
LOVE UNDERCOVER
MORTIMER HONOUR
THE HEART'S LONGING
LOVE ON SAFARI
WOMAN WITH A MISSION
BUTTERFLY LADY
SEASON OF SECRETS
A BRIDE FOR JASON
SAVE YOUR TEARS
THE SECRET HERO

WEST
DUNBARTONSHIRE
LIBRARIES

PRICE	SUPPLIER
8 -99	4
LOCATION	CLASS
AL	AF
INVOICE DATE	
ACCESSION NUMBER	
020329768	

BEVERLEY WINTER

JASPER'S TREASURE

Complete and Unabridged

LINFORD
Leicester

First published in Great Britain in 2010

First Linford Edition
published 2011

Copyright © 2010 by Beverley Winter
All rights reserved

British Library CIP Data

Winter, Beverley.
  Jasper's treasure. - -
  (Linford romance library)
  1. Fruit growers- -South Africa- -Fiction.
  2. Love stories. 3. Large type books.
  I. Title II. Series
  823.9′2–dc22

  ISBN 978–1–4448–0743–1

Published by
F. A. Thorpe (Publishing)
Anstey, Leicestershire

Set by Words & Graphics Ltd.
Anstey, Leicestershire
Printed and bound in Great Britain by
T. J. International Ltd., Padstow, Cornwall

This book is printed on acid-free paper

1

It was a beautiful morning with the sun beaming down from a clear African sky; another fine day to enjoy working in her little tea shop, Alexandra Smit reflected happily as she skipped down the stairs from her small flat above The Old Brown Teapot.

'Oh, flippin' heck!' she gasped, and stopped dead. There was an unholy mess on the floor near the door, with smashed crockery and water spilled everywhere. During the night someone had lugged a few bricks through the front window, shattering it into tiny shards which glinted like diamonds as the sunlight streamed in.

'What's happened, Lexi?' asked Gina, who had just arrived for work together with Chantal, her other assistant.

Both girls stared in dismay at the shambles before them.

'As if we don't have enough to do already,' grumbled Chantal. 'Just look at those smashed vases, and the tablecloths are absolutely ruined. What kind of person would even think to do such a terrible thing like this?'

'Some lout with nothing better to occupy his tiny mind, I suppose,' Lexi sighed. 'It doesn't look as though anything's been stolen but don't touch a thing, girls, it's a crime scene. Why not go in and start on the scones while I telephone the police? We'll have to get this lot cleared up before the glazier comes. I daresay it will take most of the morning.'

'I'm not holding my breath,' Gina said, 'because they won't find the culprit. People get away with murder in Stellenbosch these days.'

Chantal agreed. 'It gives me the creeps. We'd better watch it, ladies; they say misfortunes come in threes.'

'That's nonsense,' Lexi told them firmly, 'Nothing else bad is going to happen.' She tossed her plait of thick, silver-gold hair over one shoulder and smiled kindly at her two friends. 'Don't look so worried. It's a beautiful day and we will not allow this episode to spoil it.'

It took two hours before they could reopen the shop. Impatient customers streamed in from the street outside, eager to sample the delicious snacks Lexi and her staff had made. They particularly enjoyed the jams and relishes, and came from as far afield as Cape Town to buy them.

'Any more of that strawberry jam?' asked one woman, 'I bought two jars last month and they were gone in no time. It's marvellous; my boys are mad about it. Do you make it yourself, dear?'

'Oh, no,' Lexi smiled, taking two more jars off the shelf. 'My grand-mother makes all our jellies and preserves.'

'Fancy, now. And with fruit such a price these days . . . '

'That's not too much of a problem

3

because my grandfather grows it all on their berry farm. It's called Sunnyfields, just on the road to Franschhoek. Perhaps you may have seen the sign?'

'Can't say I have.'

Always ready to promote her grandmother's wares, she added enthusiastically, 'Have you tried this sweet-sour relish? It goes wonderfully well with venison, or barbecued fish. Oh, and cheese, too ... or would you prefer the cranberry relish?' Then she suddenly added, 'Oh, I forgot! I'd better drive out to Sunnyfields quickly.' She went into the kitchen where Gina was filling teapots and buttering scones.

'Keep an eye on things, will you? I promised to deliver the next lot of empty bottles to Gran this morning but what with the drama about the window and the glazier charging more than I'd bargained for I completely forgot about it. She's busy making strawberry jam and she'll wonder what's happened. We picked all those strawberries over the weekend and they mustn't go to waste;

there are also buckets of gooseberries still waiting in the shed. I'll try not to be long.'

'No problem, we'll manage here,' Gina assured her, adding, 'Give my love to your gran.'

She watched Lexi's departing back and gave an envious sigh. 'I wish I had her gorgeous blue eyes.'

Chantal looked up from the cream she was whipping. 'They are rather stunning, aren't they? Kind of ocean blue . . . you know how the sea is dark one minute and aqua the next? Well, when Lexi is cross they go dark.'

She ladled great dollops of cream on to the scones. 'She's a nice person, isn't she? Always so optimistic, and doesn't get uptight about things . . . like this morning.'

But Gina was determined to have a moan. 'It's not fair. Lexi seems to have everything; wonderful figure and legs that go all the way down to the South Pole.'

'But no boyfriend,' Chantal pointed

5

out. 'Perhaps it's because she's so big and strapping?' She looked down at her own petite figure with satisfaction. 'I may not be tall like Lexi — her ancestors were Dutch, you know — but at least I have plenty of admirers.'

'She did have that boyfriend a while ago but it turned out he was only after the business, so she ditched him. I must say our Lexi has her head screwed on the right way.'

'And she won't look at a man who lies.'

'And all this chatting,' Gina reminded her, 'won't get the customers fed! Are you ready with those scones?'

★ ★ ★

Henrietta, the rather dilapidated blue van which Lexi had bought with her first quarter's profits, rattled its way along the road to Franschhoek in a carefree manner, filled with the promised jars for Mrs Smit. Lexi rolled down the window and sniffed the scent-laden air from the orchards and vineyards, carried on a breeze which rustled across the wide valley. It was towered over by a stunning backdrop of mountains.

'What lovely scenery and what a perfect day,' Lexi murmured. She was a happy girl, blessed with a serene temperament which only erupted into a fiery temper when anything threatened the well-being of her beloved grandparents. 'Perfect enough,' she added firmly, 'to keep at bay any of those supposed misfortunes Chantal spoke of. Anyway, I don't believe in that sort of nonsense.'

But she spoke too soon. At that very moment the second of the day's trials reared its ugly head as Henrietta, usually a docile and co-operative companion, began to buck and wobble.

Lexi's eyes widened. 'Now what?'

With lightning speed she pulled to the side of the road and cut the engine. Fortunately the road wasn't busy at this time, having long since disposed of its quota of early traffic. She would be able to mend the puncture in peace. Punctures did not faze her. She was reared on a farm, for goodness sake! Without fuss she collected the spare tyre from its hiding place together with the tools she needed and set to work to right the problem. No problem!

It appeared to be a problem for someone else, though. The flashy red BMW coming at speed from the opposite direction screeched to a halt, executed a swift about-turn and jerked to a noisy stop just inches from Henrietta's rear bumper.

'Maniac!' she muttered crossly. What was it about men? Once they were behind the wheel of a car they felt compelled to show off at every turn.

A large man was coming towards her. He was good looking in a flashy way, with over-long dark hair and matching designer stubble which went some way to covering a slightly weak jaw. He flashed her a movie-star smile which should have had her weak at the knees but all Lexi saw were the purple trousers and expensive lilac shirt. She stifled a laugh. He looked like a bunch of lavender. So not her type!

'In trouble, lady?'

He looked her over from head to toe with pale eyes which held a certain amount of malicious glee.

Lexi's lips tightened. She didn't care for the smug tones any more than she cared to be patronised by some psychedelic male who thought the sun came up just in order to hear him crow. He was viewing her chest pointedly, too; rather like assessing the milk yield of a prize cow. She knew her figure was excellent but there was no need to ogle it in that blatant manner.

'It's nothing I can't handle,' she replied shortly. The car was already jacked up. All she needed now was a suitable wheel spanner for the nuts.

The man elbowed her aside roughly. 'Let Uncle take over, angel, I'll do the job in half the time. A female like you wouldn't know one end of a car from the other.'

Lexi choked. 'I beg your pardon?'

He added in what she considered to be a deliberate put-down, 'A woman should stick to what she knows and stay in the kitchen.' He might as well have said 'barefoot and pregnant' or 'in a man's bed'!

Lexi snatched up the spanner. The man was as unwelcome as a skunk at a picnic and any moment now she'd bite his head off for good.

'Get lost!' she muttered.

His head snapped up in disbelief. 'What did you say?'

'I said I can manage perfectly without any help,' she told him sweetly as she removed the offending wheel, reached for the spare, fitted it expertly and neatly tightened the nuts.

The man watched her, shaking his head. 'Lady, you're a freak!'

Lexi stood up, replaced her tools in the boot of her car and gave him a look to freeze his obnoxious bones. Because she'd been well brought up she thanked him for his offer of help and wished him good day, albeit curtly.

'Wait.'

Impatiently she wiped her hands on a piece of rag and tossed it into the van. 'Yes?'

She stole another look at the tall, well-built figure. He had good shoulders and a tan to die for, but a weak jaw in a man was every bit as bad as a clammy handshake. What's more, those pale eyes held a familiar, calculating expression which told her he was a man to stay away from.

'You're a large female, aren't you?' he observed, examining her splendidly built proportions with interest. 'Being large myself, I'm into females with a bit of flesh on them.'

Lexi gasped.

Ignoring her outraged face he plunged on with the sensitivity of a rhinoceros. 'Stop and have a drink with me, angel. My, er . . . family estate is just down the road. We could go there and get to know each other. You must be lonely . . . there aren't many males in these parts and I hate to see a delightful woman like you going to waste.'

Lexi took a deep breath and controlled her overwhelming desire to slap him. She needed his back-handed compliments like a pig needed perfume. 'Thank you, no,' she said politely, and slammed the door before roaring away at speed.

'Life,' she told Henrietta a moment later, 'is far too short to bother about skunks. Neither will we allow one broken window and a puncture to spoil our day, or even that silly old wives' tale about misfortunes.'

She gave a gurgle of laughter. 'However, it may yet be a case of two down, one to go!'

2

Doctor Jasper Rousseau stamped on the brake pedal and brought his silver Mercedes to a squealing halt as a small, speckled-grey animal darted across the road and disappeared into the bushes on one side.

'Look, an otter,' squeaked a small, excited voice from the back seat.

'No, son,' Jasper corrected kindly, 'that was a Cape Grey Mongoose. Herpestes pulverulentus, to be exact.'

'He forgot to look left and right before he ran across the road,' observed the four-year-old indignantly, 'We nearly ran him down.'

'Yes. Very foolish,' his father agreed gravely.

'Perhaps he was hungry. Perhaps he was running home for his dinner. What do mongooses eat, Papa?'

Jasper glanced at his small son in the

rear-view mirror. There was a warming twinkle in his steel grey eyes. 'Oh, rats, mice, lizards . . . '

'And snakes?'

'Yes, snakes, too.'

Robbie Rousseau gave a great, gusty sigh. 'Cool!' After a moment he observed thoughtfully, 'They must have very sharp teeth.'

Jasper hid a smile. At least his son was taking an interest in life again. The death of his mother six months previously had caused him to become worryingly withdrawn but constant love and discipline seemed to be restoring his sense of security. Thankfully he'd been able to give the child extra attention now that he'd resigned from his position at the university.

'I'm hungry,' Robbie announced firmly.

Carefully Jasper guided the car around a bend in the mountain pass. 'You are? What is it to be, then, lizards or snakes?'

Robbie grinned. 'I don't feel like

lizards today, Papa, or snakes.'

His father feigned surprise. 'No? I'm told they are rather tasty.'

'Ugh! I'd rather have a burger and chips, with onion rings and a banana milkshake. But no ketchup, Papa. Mama didn't like ketchup.'

She certainly hadn't. She hadn't liked marriage, either. From now on whatever Robbie lacked in a mother would have to be supplied by nannies and housekeepers because there was no way he'd tie himself to another woman. One ever-unloving spouse had been enough. It would be a lonely life but there was always his work . . .

'Right,' he agreed readily, 'A burger it is, then.' Robbie was regaining his appetite; another good sign. At one stage all he'd eat was toast and anchovy paste, his mother's favourite snack. Their holiday hadn't been in vain, then . . . all that fresh air and hours of watching dolphins and collecting small sea creatures in jars had paid off.

'Papa?'

'Yes, Robbie?''

'How much further is it to Stellenbosch?'

'Another forty minutes. Bear up like a man, son.'

As Robbie lapsed into silence Jasper was allowed a moment to brood. He still could not get his head around his unhappy past. If he ever discovered the man who'd defrauded his wife and led her astray he'd like to throttle the creep. Not that Deirdre had needed much persuasion to elope; it had been her fourth affair, but she'd done it once too often, smashing her body along with her fancy sports car. Naturally the man she'd been going to meet had disappeared into the blue yonder and the police had long since closed the file.

His grey eyes, scanning the road, were filled with remembered pain.

'Papa, why are you looking so cross?'

Jasper collected himself. He turned his handsome head and gave Robbie a reassuring smile. 'I'm not cross, son, Only sad.'

16

Robbie's mother had been a restless, discontented person, eager to be diverted from the concerns and duties of domesticity and motherhood. When he'd married her he thought he'd found his heart's treasure. It hadn't taken him long to discover that the gem was 'paste'. Even so, she'd been young and beautiful and she hadn't deserved to die.

'Are we going home to the wine farm afterwards, Papa?' asked Robbie, who liked to know what was happening.

'Maison Rousseau? Yes.' The beautiful estate he'd recently inherited from his uncle, Jacques Rousseau, and established by his French Huguenot forbears. Intrepid and God-fearing vintners, they had fled a Europe torn by religious strife and brought their precious cultivars with them. Greatly helped by the excellent climate and unique soils, the vineyard still continued to produce wines of great quality.

'Papa,' Robbie asked suddenly, gazing out of the window, 'Are there baboons in these mountains?'

'There certainly are. Why not see if you can spot a troupe of them?' And because he'd made wild animals his life's study, added under his breath, 'Papio ursinus . . . '

The Mercedes continued to nose its way through the mountains but Robbie wasn't interested in baboons; he had other things on his mind.

'Will they have chocolate chip cookies, Papa?'

'Who, the baboons?'

Robbie chuckled. The unexpected sound was music in his father's ears. 'No, silly. The place where we're going to eat.'

Jasper, who was not accustomed to frequenting fast food establishments, was momentarily at a loss.

'Er, I have no idea, Robbie. Anything's possible.'

The ocean appeared on their left, that thirty-kilometre stretch of sparkling water known as False Bay, with its wide beaches so beloved of summer bathers.

18

Jasper pressed on through the town of Somerset West and headed north to Stellenbosch, intent on feeding his son.

'Where in heaven's name do we find a burger?' he murmured, cruising the streets of the university town renowned for its ancient oak trees and old-world architecture. The sun had disappeared behind the Helderberg Mountain by the time they re-emerged, having eaten to Robbie's satisfaction apart from the chocolate chip cookies, of which there'd been none available.

'Never mind, son,' Jasper consoled him, 'We'll ask Mrs Kama to make us a batch tomorrow.'

Robbie heaved a great sigh. 'Our housekeeper is not a very good cook, is she, Papa?'

Jasper grinned, remembering the beef stew and inedible dumplings they'd been forced to consume on occasion. 'No, but there's no harm in asking. Like I said, anything's possible.'

By the time they had reached Maison Rousseau, that gracious homestead standing in white-washed splendour among the vines, Robbie had fallen asleep. The car slid to a halt on the wide sweep of gravel outside the house with its impressive entrance, thatched roof and many-paned windows flanked by dark green shutters.

Jasper carried his son across the veranda flagstones, ducking his head under one of the low hanging vines beside the door. They had arrived home a day earlier than scheduled and he did not expect his staff to be in attendance. He unlocked the yellowwood door, darkened by time to a rich honey colour, and shoved it open with one broad shoulder.

In the soft amber glow of the lamp in the hall he carried his son up the carved oak staircase to the bedroom and tucked him under his much-loved Spiderman duvet. Hopefully Robbie would not be disturbed by any of the bad dreams he'd suffered since Deirdre's death.

'Goodnight, my boy,' he said softly as

he arranged the two teddy bears, Toast and Honey, beside the sleeping child.

As he went to fetch in the luggage he was completely unaware that his own nightmare, albeit of a different kind, was about to begin.

3

The blue van with its load of bottles turned off the main road at the sign saying Sunnyfields Berry Farm. 'The raspberries are looking good,' Lexi murmured as she bumped up the dusty drive past the terraces of fruit and pulled up with a jerk behind her grandparents' pretty whitewashed cottage. 'Gran . . . ?' she called out.

'In here, love.' Her grandmother's voice, normally cheery and upbeat, sounded oddly subdued.

Lexi's head jerked up. Surely this couldn't be misfortune number three rearing its tiresome head? Curious but not exactly anxious, she composed her features into a friendly calm and headed down the passage.

'Is anything wrong?'

Her diminutive grandmother was sitting in her favourite pink armchair looking smaller than ever. She fumbled for her lace-edged handkerchief and daintily blew her nose, looking helplessly at her husband.

'Perhaps we had better tell her, Johannes,' she quavered.

Lexi looked from one to the other with growing concern and worry. 'Tell me what? What's happened?' Her grandfather's tired old face looked drawn with tension.

'What is it you must tell me, Grandpa? Are you ill?'

'No, child, I am not ill. Your grandmother is a little upset, that's all. It is nothing which need concern you.'

'Rubbish! Gran doesn't cry for nothing and you know perfectly well that whatever it is, we're all in it together.' She paused. 'May I remind you there is such a thing as family solidarity? You've cared for me since the age of six when Mom and Dad died and you sent me to the best private school in Cape Town. You even raided your savings to help me start my business. I owe you both big time, and you know it. So bring it on. What's happened? I'm a great, strapping girl of twenty-four. You have no need to protect me.'

'You are quite right,' Mrs Smit sniffed, 'We ought not to keep our woes from you. Tell her, Johannes'

Mr Smit sighed. 'We had a visit from our landlord this morning.' He shook his head in disbelief, 'A very unpleasant individual indeed.'

Lexi stared. 'You mean old Jacques Rousseau? But he's always been rather a dear.'

'No, Lexi. Jacques died recently, did we not tell you? Apparently a nephew is now the owner of Maison Rousseau.'

'So? What has that got to do with us?'

'He wants the land back,' her grandmother blurted with a small sob. 'He was the most arrogant young man I have ever encountered. He bullied us and threatened us and even laughed at our distress, in our very faces.' She added indignantly, 'He had pale fish-eyes and they were a little too close together, too . . . '

Lexi's fine brows drew together in a frown. 'I don't understand.'

Her grandfather proceeded to enlighten her. 'He told us our lease is invalid now that the estate is under new ownership.'

'But that's ridiculous! A lease is a legal document and therefore binding.'

Mr Smit's chest heaved. 'Even so, the new owner is entitled to do as he wishes. He has given us a month's notice. He says he has other uses for the land and we must move out by Christmas. If we do not comply he will triple the rent until we do. Obviously we would be unable to cope.'

His breathing had become alarmingly laboured. Any moment now, thought Lexi, he would have another of his asthma attacks.

'And what is to become of our orchard?' her grandmother wailed, making a valiant effort to control her trembling lips. 'The b-berries . . . all our hard work . . . we will not be able to harvest them and your business will suffer and what about our part time gardeners? They won't be able to get other jobs so easily around here.' She burst into fresh sobs, 'Oh, dear, we are too old to move . . . '

Lexi jumped up. 'A nice cup of redbush tea is what we all need, along with a piece of chocolate cake. It's called comfort food, and quite rightly so.' She bent to kiss her grandfather's cheek. 'I'll be right back with your inhaler, Grandpa. We'll have our tea and then decide what is to be done. Try not to worry darlings, it will turn out for the best, you'll see.'

Sounding calmer than she felt, she pinned a smile on her face to hide the mounting rage inside her. Not given to irate outbursts she nevertheless slammed about the kitchen muttering furiously under her breath.

'That man is unspeakable!' she stormed, momentarily startling her grandmother's ginger cat, Sawdust, who was sunning himself peacefully on the windowsill. He then took not the slightest notice, once more closing his green eyes upon the world.

By this time Lexi had worked herself into quite a state. 'There is no way he will get away with this, the money-grubbing toad! I intend to force him. back into his slimy pond!'

She took a deep breath to calm her shaking hands and knotted insides, trying at the same time to be reasonable. Naturally the man could do what he liked with his own property, but there was such a thing as honouring an agreement made in good faith. There was also such a thing as showing a little compassion to an elderly couple, especially as they had been good tenants for a number of years, always paying on the dot and never giving cause for complaint.

'There you are my dears,' she said as she poured the tea and handed round her grandmother's favourite cake plate. At the same time she chatted lightly about inconsequential nothings until they began to relax. It was only as she dried up the tea things that she remembered what Gran had said and almost dropped the treasured china.

'Pale eyes . . . '

'Of course!' she whispered. 'Why didn't I think of it before?' Their new landlord was the frightful man she'd met on the road. Hadn't he told her his estate was nearby? She felt quite sick at the thought. But much as she hated to see that tanned, stubbled face again she refused to back down from a confrontation. She'd go across to Maison Rousseau as soon as possible and demand that he see reason.

Carefully she replaced the cups, smiling nastily. The skunk would find out he wasn't the only one capable of causing a stink!

★   ★   ★

Just as the sun was peeping over the oak trees Mrs Maria Kama, housekeeper par excellence in her own happy estimation and wife of Jakob the head gardener, negotiated the well-worn pathway from their tiny cottage on the estate, and entered the kitchen.

'Good morning, Gerda,' she greeted her assistant, 'I'm glad to see you are busy with the breakfast.' She nodded her colourful scarf-bedecked head in satisfaction. 'The master is back; he arrived last night.'

Gerda's brown face broke into a smile. 'Yes, I know, Mrs Kama. I heard the little boy playing in his bedroom when I came in.' She stirred the oatmeal porridge and enquired respect-fully of her superior, 'Would the master like bacon or sausages with the eggs?'

'Grill the bacon and leave the sausages for his lunch. The master is a big man. He needs a lot of feeding, just like my Jakob.' She picked up the tray Gerda had prepared. 'You get on while I take in his tea. He likes it in the study because he always works for an hour before breakfast.' She added in an admiring voice laced with motherly indulgence, 'He's a very hard worker, is the master.'

Jasper looked up from his computer as though he had never seen her before; his mind had been grappling with oak barrels, cellar temperatures and modern stainless steel tanks with gravity flow . . .

'Good morning, sir. Did you and Master Robbie have a good holiday?'

'Yes, very pleasant, thank you, Maria. Did everything go smoothly here in my absence?'

Mrs Kama's beam faltered. Her wrinkled brown face, a legacy of her Hottentot heritage, revealed her concern. 'Yes, sir. Everything except . . . '

Jasper, a highly perceptive man, noted the well-concealed anger. His gaze sharpened.

'Except what?'

'Master Roger arrived,' she admitted in an unhappy voice.

'Ah . . . ' His dark brows drew together in a frown. That explained things. His obnoxious cousin had been upsetting the staff again.

'He came this morning, sir. He stayed for an hour and then went away again.' The housekeeper closed her mouth with a snap. It wouldn't do to tell the master how he had fished about for ages amongst the desk papers and then shouted for tea just when there were no scones in the house. He'd been very rude, too, demanding this and that and never a word of thanks.

'What did my cousin want?'

'I don't know, sir. He said he'd come back and see you at four o'clock. He was very angry.'

'I see. Thank you, Maria.' As the housekeeper turned to go he added kindly, 'Tell Jakob I'm very pleased with the garden. The hydrangeas are looking wonderful.'

Her beam returned. The master was a considerate and courteous employer just like his uncle before him. It was a good thing Master Roger had not inherited the estate because she and

Jakob would have handed in their notice.

Roger Rousseau's red BMW roared up the drive two hours later than stipulated. He marched into the house, flung down car keys and stalked down the passage.

' 'Where the flaming heck have you been?' he demanded.

Jasper, temper well in hand, ushered him into the small sitting room at the back of the house. Once used by Tante Magda, Jacques Rousseau's wife, it was a cosy room, furnished in pale blue velvet with a great many photographs in silver frames on the bureau. Large French windows, suitably draped and tasselled, opened on to a well-tended rose garden.

'On holiday, as you full well know,' Jasper replied shortly. 'What can I do for you, Roger? I'm told you have already been making free with my home in my absence.'

'Your home? By rights it damned well should have been mine!' Roger's features twisted in fury, 'I'm older than you are. It should have been me that inherited the estate.'

Jasper's grey eyes turned steely. 'We've been through all this before, Roger. However, I'll say it one more time. Uncle Jacques was entitled to leave Maison Rousseau to whomever he wished. Yes, we are both his nephews since our fathers were his brothers and yes, you are the eldest amongst the cousins. But this fact did not automatically entitle you to inherit. You received a generous legacy from Uncle Jacques, as did the others. Why can't you be satisfied with that?'

Roger gave a harsh laugh. 'That piffling amount? You call that a decent inheritance? It didn't last long. You don't seem to understand that my lifestyle requires cash.'

'Oh, I understand very well,' Jasper responded dryly. His cousin had an extravagant and irresponsible streak and was all too often the author of his own misfortunes.

'The truth is, Roger, had you shown more prudence over the years Uncle Jacques may well have left you the estate. But he left it to me and I intend to hand it on to my son, having built on a very fine heritage; it's what Jacques would have wanted. And now, cousin, be good enough to depart. I've had a very long day and my housekeeper is waiting to serve dinner.'

Roger heaved himself off the sofa and rudely helped himself to Jasper's glass of wine, slamming down the empty crystal as though it were plastic.

'Not so fast, cousin!' he grated, his eyes hard. 'There is still the matter of the portion he promised me when I was fifteen years old.'

Jasper's eyebrows rose in disbelief. 'What portion?'

Roger's pale eyes gleamed with spite. 'The ten acres known as Sunnyfields.' He spat out the name as though it were an obscenity. 'I'm referring to the land next door, Jasper, currently rented to those two old bats who play around with fruit bushes. There's a snooty blonde piece with long legs who visits them.' Still smarting from his lack of success that morning, he sneered, 'The woman drives a clapped out old van like a she-demon and won't give a decent man the time of day.'

Jasper racked his brains. 'You mean the Smits?'

'The same. A promise is a promise, Jasper. Uncle Jacques meant me to have that land and you are morally bound to give it to me.'

'I'll do no such thing,' Jasper said firmly. 'There was nothing in the will. You're lying.'

'I want that land, Jasper, and I mean to have it. I already have a buyer, a developer who wants to put up holiday lets and a mall with a movie house and casino. This dump needs livening up.'

Jasper stared at his cousin in disbelief. The man actually wanted to despoil an area of incredible natural beauty; the whole valley would be ruined. It was akin to rape.

'You're mad,' he said coldly.

Roger shrugged. He stubbed out his cigarette in one of Tante Magda's prized Delft bowls and shrugged into his mustard-coloured jacket, a tasteless garment which he fancied went well with the purple trousers. The ruse, he thought angrily, had not worked. Jasper was a hard nut but he, Roger, wasn't beaten yet.

'Well, if you won't give it to me outright then at least lease it to me.' He had certain other plans up his sleeve. It would be an easy matter to drive a couple of old loonies away and at the same time he'd show the blonde bimbo a thing or two about male authority.

'No, I will not lease you the land.'

'We'll see about that,' Roger sniggered. Jasper would be forced to eat his words because he, Roger, wasn't a good estate agent for nothing. He knew a thing or two about wheeling and dealing. He didn't really have a developer; he'd just said that to wind old Jasper up. He had something completely different in mind and he stood to make a good deal of money from it. He'd sub-lease the land to that special client who wished to remain anonymous. The man had promised to let him in on the operation and not even the police would suspect a thing; the area was too isolated.

'You're a fool in more ways than one, Jasper,' he taunted, 'A blind, sightless fool.' Hadn't it been an easy matter to seduce his dolly-bird of a wife under his very nose? It was a pity the woman had crashed her car; they were about to have fun together . . .

With a smirk Roger turned away. 'I'll be going now. I'll see my lawyer about a lease for the property and be in touch.' He slammed the front door on his way out.

Jasper, not a man normally given to swearing, uttered something sharp under his breath. He could see that Roger hadn't changed a bit; always making trouble and blaming someone else. He was obviously cooking up something shady, if not downright illegal. The man was as slippery as a greased pig and just as greedy.

'And I daresay I haven't heard the last of it.' Jasper sighed as he took himself to the dining room for his dinner.

'I'll take my coffee in the study, thank you, Maria,' he told the housekeeper afterwards. He went down the passage, intending to take another look at the leasing arrangement for Sunnyfields Berry Farm.

'Of course, sir.'

Mrs Kama was on her way back to the kitchen when she heard the sound of a motor car racing through the vines. Another visitor! She'd better make a larger pot of coffee and set a second cup on the tray.

At that moment Gerda, clearing the table in the dining room, peered out of the window.

'There's a blue van outside,' she announced as she came back into the kitchen a moment later, 'and a very cross looking lady is climbing out.'

4

Despite her anger Lexi was curious to see Maison Rousseau. She climbed out of the van, unprepared for its magnificence. The historic old house with its gracious ambience and beautiful mountain backdrop was particularly beautiful. As for the vineyard she'd just driven through, it contained some of the finest of red cultivars she'd ever seen. The vines looked healthy, too; acres of lush greenery bursting with ripening grapes which would produce some of the best Chardonnay, Shiraz and Merlot wines in the country.

Old Jacques Rousseau had certainly known what he was about . . . which brought her to the odious nephew, who obviously did not when it came to human relationships.

Lexi stamped across the veranda resolving to fight every inch of the way in order to protect their rights. What's more, if the skunk knew any prayers, now was the time to say them because she was about to cut out his gizzard and feed it to her grandmother's cat.

Ruthlessly she grasped the solid brass knocker and hammered on the door. It did little to relieve her feelings.

Mrs Kama answered the summons and stared.

'Good evening, Miss.' The master hadn't had a visit from such a pretty young lady before, but she looked as though she'd swallowed a bee; Jakob had told her there were plenty about in the garden at the moment.

'Good evening, I would like to see your employer,' Lexi stated, politely but firmly.

'Come in and I will inform Doctor Rousseau that you are here. Please wait.' She waddled off importantly, leaving Lexi fretting in the hallway. So he had a doctorate, she reflected. Well, educated or not, he was an arrogant man with absolutely no manners.

'Doctor Rousseau will see you now Miss,' Mrs Kama announced a moment later, 'Please follow me.'

Nervously Lexi fingered her grandparents' lease agreement in the pocket of her denim skirt. At the study door she paused to fling back her bright curtain of hair. The plait she'd worn all day had come loose at the last minute and she'd opted to leave it loose, but its thick waves were a great nuisance when not tied back.

Mrs Kama nodded her head encouragingly and returned to the kitchen for that tray of coffee. She would add a plate of chocolate biscuits just to show the young lady that the master had everything of the best.

Lexi looked up and her eyes widened in amazement. Her pretty mouth fell open as she stared in confusion at the gorgeous hunk who had risen from the desk. He was regarding her through narrowed, slate-grey eyes which were not entirely friendly at this moment. They were stunning eyes, she thought wildly, not pale and definitely not too close together; on the contrary they were nicely spaced and fringed with thick lashes under a pair of dark, well-shaped brows.

The man took his time, looking her over with an impassive face. Although seemingly indifferent, he was by no means immune to what he saw.

Lexi gazed at him, unable to utter a single word. He was a very large man, tall and broad, with excellent legs encased in navy denims. A crisp white shirt strained across his shoulders and barely concealed the well-defined musculature beneath; it was unfastened at the neck to reveal a strong, tanned throat and his jaw was certainly not weak, it was positively tough. His dark hair was fashionably cut, threaded slightly with silver and curling on his neck in a heart-stopping manner.

For no reason Lexi could define, that organ began to hammer against her startled ribs so that she was forced to take a deep, calming breath as she tried to reassess the situation.

'G-good evening,' she stammered at length, astonished at her own reaction. Despite her size she felt very small and vulnerable when confronted with all that virile masculinity. The person now viewing her with detached interest was obviously no slouch. He was obviously not the man she had come to see! Had there been some horrible mistake?

Lexi gathered her senses and drew herself up in a haughty manner so as not to reveal how threatened she felt. At all costs she must try to appear unfazed and in control.

Doctor Rousseau continued to observe her steadily. The woman was curiously bereft of words, so he felt compelled to prompt in a deep voice which held a slight rasp, 'Good evening. You wished to see me?'

'Um . . . '

A gleam of amusement appeared in the grey eyes, just as though he were well aware of the effect he had on women. He was not a conceited man, well used to fending off the besotted hero worship of the female students who had plagued him at the university, but he would not be human if he did not enjoy her reaction. So he merely waited.

By this time Lexi had become considerably rattled. Her thoughts tumbled erratically in her confused mind. He was not the man she'd come to accost — and no other man had ever affected her like this. She felt like a caterpillar on a leaf, waiting to be consumed by some great, horrid bird.

'And yet . . . ' she whispered. And yet he must surely be as big a scoundrel as the other. Anyone could see they were in it together. Filled with sudden rage she blurted in a shrill, angry voice, 'Where is he? Where's the man with the fish-eyes and the undershot jaw?'

Jasper's own jaw dropped. 'Er . . . '

'Your accomplice,' she grated, 'Where is he? I wish to speak with him at once.' His astonishment, instantly concealed behind a bland mask, served only to

44

increase her fury. 'Don't bother to deny it,' she stormed. 'The two of you ought to be ashamed of yourselves! You may be a handsome man — I'll not deny it — but you're a handsome toad! Just like the other one. Actually,' she amended wildly, 'the other one was more like a disgusting bullfrog and he called me 'big'. Well, I might be, but I'm proud of it, and I have come to make you both see sense. Be assured you will not get away with this, you unscrupulous pair of — of — skunks!'

Quite carried away by her strong feelings her charming bosom began to heave, a sight noted by Jasper in some appreciation. She was astonishingly beautiful, with amazing hair and eyes like two great, flashing sapphires. It was a pity she was unhinged.

'Mad as a hatter,' he muttered under his breath.

Uncaring, Lexi plunged on. 'You will retract your outrageous demands on my grandparents, is that clear?'

He folded his arms across his chest

with the air of a man who was preparing to enjoy himself. 'As mud.'

Lexi's glare became positively ferocious. 'The other toad paid a visit to them yesterday,' she hissed, 'as you well know. He was thoroughly awful, bullying them and threatening them and laughing at them.' She gulped for breath. 'They are extremely upset and I won't have it! Grandmother said his eyes were too c-close together . . . ' To her utter mortification her mouth wobbled.

'I see,' Jasper nodded, greatly entertained behind his calm mask. She was definitely loco. In a moment he'd be forced to telephone for the men in the white coats.

'I advise you to change your mind and withdraw before I am forced to take legal action,' Lexi added in a shrill voice. Even in her own ears she sounded like a fishwife but she was beyond caring.

Not a muscle on Jasper's face moved. All the same she was aware that he was laughing his head off. 'Legal action..?' he coaxed.

'It's no laughing matter!'

'No, I dare say it isn't,' he agreed calmly. 'Will you not sit down?'' He indicated a brown leather armchair, unable to keep his gaze from her hair; it was not quite silver and not quite gold and reminded him of a field of ripe wheat in the moonlight.

Lexi took a deep breath and looked at him sternly. 'No thank you, I prefer to stand while I'm doing business.'

Jasper choked. 'We're doing business?'

'What else do you think I'm here for? What are you going to do about the situation, that's what I'd like to know?'

'I take it,' Jasper said slowly, 'that you are referring to those . . . er . . . outrageous demands?'

'You know exactly what I'm referring to so kindly do not play dumb,' she snapped. 'I have it here in my pocket and like I said I will see my lawyer if we do not get any satisfaction from you

47

and your accomplice.'

Jasper's mouth twitched. 'Forgive me, but I have no idea to what you are referring. Be good enough to explain. What is it that you have in your pocket? A handkerchief? A tube of lipstick? Allow me to say that your complexion is that good, you surely have no need of any embellishments.' He eyed her from his great height, thoroughly enjoying the circus. It made a nice change from his cousin's ranting.

Lexi's mouth fell open. She closed it with a snap. 'The lease, damn you,' she exploded, 'and there is no need to be so patronising.'

He was looking genuinely puzzled. 'Lease? What lease, lady? Who exactly are you?' Lexi ground her splendid teeth. 'You're playing dumb again. The lease for the acreage we use, of course — for the land you want to use for other purposes.' She fished it out of her pocket and waved it at him. 'See here, Mister — Doctor — or whoever you are. Allow me to remind you that it's a legal document. It says that this is valid indefinitely. That means for as long as we want it. We cannot be evicted from Sunnyfields Berry Farm, no matter what you wish to do with the land.'

Jasper's amusement dropped off instantly and his eyes widened in sudden comprehension. He held up one hand. 'Wait. I take it you are one of the Smit family?'

'You take it correctly. I am Alexandra Smit and you know perfectly well that my grandparents, Johannes and Marta Smit, have been your Uncle's loyal tenants for years, always paying their rent on time and never giving cause for complaint. It is very cruel of you to kick them out now, and without any warning.'

Jasper went very still. He gave her a long, hard stare. 'Let's get this straight. Am I given to understand there is some problem with the lease and that someone has told your grandparents it is invalid and that they must leave?' He shook his head as if to clear it. The crazy woman was beginning to make sense at last.

Lexi was speechless at his stalling tactics. When she recovered she rounded on him wrathfully.

'Problem? Of course there is a problem! Your obnoxious partner called and threatened my grandparents in a very cruel manner. Wouldn't you say there was a problem when you have both been so crass as to kick them out of their home and tell them they must get going by Christmas? I'd definitely call that a problem!' She mistook his suddenly grim expression for opposition and persisted tightly, as though it explained everything, 'He is an arrogant man and his eyes are pale and . . . ' close to tears, she gulped, 'and he l-laughed at them.'

Jasper's own eyes turned iron hard. Roger! It was just the sort of unspeakable thing he would do. He was up to something nasty and it was obvious he'd incensed these poor people. Yet again it was left to him to clean up the mess in the pigpen.

'I think we should be able to sort this out, Miss Smit. There has been a regrettable misunderstanding.'

'Some misunderstanding!' Lexi muttered.

'May I offer you a cup of coffee?' Without waiting for a reply Jasper stuck his head out of the study and yelled for Mrs Kama. That lady, who had been listening at the door only moments earlier, appeared in a rush from the kitchen, tray in hand.

'Yes, sir, the coffee is ready.' She placed the tray on Jasper's desk, at the same time managing a thorough scrutiny of the visitor. The young lady had had a lot of war words with the master and was now looking as though she'd been struck by lightning. The master would know what to do. The master always knew what to do. She must remember to tell Jakob all about it later tonight.

While Jasper poured coffee into the

mugs Lexi persisted in her attack, scorn lacing her tones. 'How can there have been a misunderstanding? The man was very definite about it. By Christmas, he said.'

Jasper gave a frustrated sigh. His bland reply gave nothing away of the sudden rage inside him.

'I daresay he was, Miss Smit. I regret to say that my cousin, Roger Rousseau, was completely out of line. I'm afraid he wants the land for his own use and acted without my knowledge or permission. Please accept my profound apology.'

'I see,' said Lexi, who definitely did not.

Jasper handed her a cup. 'Sugar?'

'No thank you. Please continue with your oh-so-interesting explanation.'

Jasper winced. He owed the Smits a more complete explanation, embarrassing though it might be. At every turn Roger appeared intent on tarnishing the family name.

He cleared his throat. 'I recently

inherited Maison Rousseau which now belongs to me in its entirety. That includes the portion your grandparents rent, Miss Smit. My cousin had no right to visit you. It only remains for me yet again to offer my sincere apologies. Please tell your grandparents that I deeply regret their distress, and that the lease still stands. I have no intention of 'kicking them out of their home', as you put it, and if they have any further queries I would be happy to address them.'

Lexi took a deep breath and closed her eyes in relief. 'Oh,' she said in a small voice. Doctor Rousseau's actions had taken all the wind from her sails. There was no longer any threat to her grandparents. 'Thank you,'' she repeated earnestly as a radiant smile transformed her cross face, 'Thank you very much.'

Feeling the need to make herself scarce before he changed his mind, she drained her cup and set it down on the table beside an untidy pile of books, all of which appeared to be about viticulture.

Perhaps Doctor Rousseau wasn't such a toad after all. Not, she told herself fiercely, that she ever wanted to set eyes on him again. Unable to help herself, she gazed at him with great blue eyes and remarked ingenuously, 'I'm glad it wasn't you, you know. It couldn't have been you, could it? Your eyes are just right, if I may say so.' Jasper submitted to her careful scrutiny of his features in silent amusement, even more entertained when she blurted forthrightly, 'Your cousin has appalling taste in clothes. But your clothes are very suitable, if rather dull.'

'Thank you for the few kind words. And now, if there is nothing else . . . ?'

'Nothing at all,' she agreed, at her most gracious.

'Then my housekeeper will see you out.' He held out a hand. 'Goodbye, Miss Smit.'

Lexi took his hand, disconcerted to find that his clasp was firm, warm and

54

reassuring. So much so that she found herself wanting to throw herself against that wide chest and feel forever safe; a foolish notion if ever there was one — and she a sensible Dutch girl!

'Thank you for the coffee,' she clipped, suddenly shy. 'Goodnight.'

'Wait.'

She turned. 'Yes?'

Jasper hesitated, seeking the right words. It was a long time since he had paid a woman a compliment and it made him feel very old.

'Your hair, Miss Smit . . . it's er . . . it's very beautiful.' Even as he spoke he felt like a lovesick schoolboy. What had possessed him to say a thing like that? He must have had a rush of blood to the head. He, a cynical old bachelor in his mid thirties, definitely past his sell-by date and father to a young child.

Lexi looked surprised. 'Is it? Well . . . thank you.' She paused. 'I'm not really an angry person, you know. I'm sorry I was so rude but you see I don't stand for my grandparents being messed about. It makes me want to do what my forefathers always did — they were Voortrekkers, you know — they circled the wagons when they were attacked in the veld. They were fierce fighters. They had to be, to survive.' She bit her lip at the thought. 'I suppose it's because Gran and Grandpa are the only family I have left that I always try to protect them.'

'And quite right, too. I would feel the same way.'

Jasper looked down at her, reassuringly large; the epitome of kindness and security, and thought about the extent to which he, too, would go to go to protect his own.

'You would? Oh . . . well, that's all right, then.' Lexi's smile was so brilliant that he blinked.

'It certainly is. Good night, Miss Smit.'

Jasper stared at her departing back, completely disarmed. He returned to his chair and sat alone with his thoughts for a considerable time before rousing himself to pour another mug of coffee. By this time the pot was cold. He gave up in disgust and returned to his computer, opened the estate records and found the Smits' file. He perused it briefly and closed it again with a frustrated sigh. Meeting the beautiful, crazy, endearing Miss Alexandra Smit had disrupted his whole evening and, he suspected, his future well-ordered existence. He felt like a frog in a blender; unsettled, to say the least.

* * *

'Papa, what are we going to do today?' Robbie asked at breakfast.

'We're driving to Stellenbosch to speak to the lady who runs the nursery school, remember? We're going to enrol you, and perhaps she will allow you to start as soon as possible.' Much as he loved his small son, he could ill afford the time to amuse him.

Robbie looked doubtful. 'Will I like it there?'

'I'm sure you will, son. You'll make plenty of new friends and be able to play with all the toys in the garden. I daresay they'll have scooters and tricycles and footballs . . . you'd like that.'

'Is that the school next to the picture of the brown teapot?'

Jasper stared at his son for a moment before he understood. 'Oh, you mean that tea shop in Church Street? Yes, that's the one.'

At Robbie's continued uncertainty he coaxed, 'Would you like to visit the tea shop afterwards? We'll find out if they have any chocolate chip cookies. Now finish your porridge because we need to get going.'

Forty minutes later Jasper's Mercedes cruised past the various curio and antique shops in the town and parked in a space near Mountain Monkeys Play School. They were welcomed by the headmistress, Miss Marsh, and ushered into her office.

'Do you have any chocolate chip

cookies at this school?' Robbie asked as soon as the details of his application had been discussed.

Stella Marsh smiled. 'I'm afraid not, Robbie, but I'm sure my friend who owns the tea shop next door will have some. She's a very good cook. Why don't you ask her?' She saw them to the door nodded goodbye and added, 'We look forward to seeing you tomorrow, Robbie.'

Robbie gave her a shy smile. 'Okay. I guess the lady next door will know how to make them because Mrs Kama sure can't.' He added in an aggrieved little voice, 'She doesn't hardly know how to make anything!'

Jasper hid a smile, thanked Miss Marsh for allowing his son to start school the next day and ushered Robbie into the tea shop. Bright gingham checks covered all the tables and pretty vases of summer flowers graced their centres. Jasper seated his son and looked around at the cheery yellow decor, annoyed to find himself thinking of a magnificent head of silvery-gold hair which hung down its owner's back like a shining waterfall. Miss Alexandra Smit, who had visited him at Maison Rousseau the previous evening, had not been out of his thoughts for a single moment.

Then he looked up and did a double-take. Miss Smit was beaming down at him, pencil and notebook in hand, waiting for his order.

Jasper rose politely and stared like an idiot. 'Miss Smit,' he managed, 'What are you doing here?'

Lexi laughed. 'I won't ask you the same, Doctor Rousseau, because you have obviously come to sample our fine wares.' She added proudly, 'This is my little business, and we have — '

'Where are your chocolate chip cookies?' Robbie interrupted, eyeing the counter area with childish urgency, 'Miss Marsh said that you had chocolate chip cookies.' When he failed to see them he explained anxiously, 'That's why we've come.'

Lexi frowned. 'Oh, dear. There are none at present, I'm afraid. We will only be baking them this afternoon when things calm down a bit. Would you like something else instead? We have scones, milk tart and carrot cake.'

Robbie looked mutinous. He thrust out his bottom lip as a small tear trickled from the corner of one blue eye. He shook his dark head and said firmly, 'I only eat chocolate chip cookies.'

Jasper sighed. Surely Robbie was not going to be difficult about food again? He gave Lexi a quick glance which hid a thorough perusal of the long, shapely legs beneath her short, business-like black skirt. The waterfall of her hair from last night had been ruthlessly suppressed into a thick rope but one or two tendrils of gold had escaped and were feathering her pink-flushed cheeks.

'May we have a pot of tea, a glass of orange juice and two of your scones? I'm sure they're excellent.'

'They are,' Lexi agreed proudly. My grandmother makes all our jellies and jams. The fruit is home grown . . . at Sunnyfields, of course.'

She noticed that the small boy was valiantly controlling his sobs. 'Is this your son, Doctor Rousseau?' What an adorable child, she thought, but where was the wife?

'Yes, this is Robbie. Unfortunately he had set his heart on those cookies but I'm sure a scone will be fine.'

Lexi's soft heart became even softer. 'Would you like me to bring you some of our cookies when they are baked, Robbie? I know where you live, and it would be no trouble at all since I have to visit my grandparents after work, anyway.'

Robbie perked up like magic and dashed the tears from his cheeks. 'Yes please.' He looked happily at his father. 'Isn't she a nice lady, Papa?'

Jasper's face was impassive. 'Very nice, Robbie, but I don't think we should impose on Miss Smit — '

'That's settled then,' Lexi intervened firmly. She would drop off her grandmother's groceries and then deliver the cookies. Besides, she was curious to see the wife. She was bound to be a fashion plate; one of those real eyeball pleasers. Even Robbie was a nice looking child.

'About six o'clock, then?'

'That would be fine,' Jasper agreed, 'It's most kind of you, Miss Smit.' Then to his own astonishment he heard himself adding, 'Perhaps you would care to stay and dine with us?'

Lexi's eyes widened. 'Well . . . that is very kind, but should you not to ask your wife first?'

Jasper's lips tightened and his eyes narrowed. 'Robbie's mother will not be present,' he said shortly.

'Oh. In that case I don't think I will. I mean, if it were me . . . '

His voice turned silky. 'If it were you . . . ?'

Lexi went faintly pink. 'Well, I wouldn't let my husband invite strange ladies to the house in my absence . . . I mean . . . ' the pink turned to red, 'It wouldn't be right, if you see what I mean?'

Jasper's eyes became very grey. 'What a delightfully old fashioned girl you are, Miss Smit. However, allow me to put your mind at rest. There is no Mrs Rousseau.'

Lexi swallowed, feeling like a great fool, along with sudden delight. 'Oh.'

'So you see, Miss Smit, I am not the erring husband you imagine me to be, any more than I am that — toad, I think you said? Or was it skunk? My memory fails me.'

Lexi met his twinkling eyes with a composed air and a racing heart which thumped madly against her ribcage.

'Take your pick, I'm not bothered. But about dinner,' she told him primly, 'I should be pleased to accept.' She made a great show of clearing the table, flicking away several imaginary crumbs with her duster. 'And my name,' she added, allowing her thick, curling lashes to sweep her overheated cheeks, 'is Lexi.'

She stood staring after him. What a strange man he was. Friendly one minute and bland as whitewash the next. When he wasn't being stern, that is. He'd got up and left in a tearing hurry, too. Was it something she'd said?

5

Roger Rousseau left the law firm offices situated next door to his estate agency and headed for the parking lot. He smirked as he glanced down at his brown leather briefcase. In it lay the lease agreement for Sunnyfields Berry Farm, which his stuffy, righteous cousin would be forced to sign before the month was out. There was no way Jasper would be allowed to interfere with the neatly laid plans he and Jan Theron had been cogitating over for months.

He climbed into the red BMW and drove to a suburb on the outskirts of Stellenbosch where he pulled up before an imposing mansion set in emerald lawns bordered by bright summer flowers and neat shrubs. A large, sparkling swimming pool with its splashing fountain graced the lawn near a weeping willow tree and on its slate surround were several reclining chairs and marble-topped tables.

'Money,' Roger muttered enviously, 'Trust Jan Theron to know how to make it by the bucket load.'

He brightened when he thought of their proposed venture. In a few months he, Roger Rousseau, would be rolling in dough till it was coming out of his ears — if all went well and he could get hold of that land. It would be ideal for what they had in mind, too; warm, sunny and bright, as well as being off the beaten track. And the soil was rich; a grower's dream. It was frustrating to have to wait on Jasper's say-so, damn him!

He rang the bell and was ushered inside by an African housemaid neatly attired in a bright green overall and matching headscarf. She led him down the spacious hallway and tapped nervously on a door.

'Come,' Jan Theron's voice rasped. That gentleman, overweight and almost completely bald, was lounging in a great leather armchair, smoking a cigar. He didn't bother to stand up but merely motioned for Roger to be seated and indicated the half dozen bottles of vintage champagne standing on a side table.

'Help yourself,' he growled. The action caused his double chin to wobble alarmingly.

'Why are we celebrating so early?' Roger asked in a sour tone, 'The cat's not in the bag yet. In other words, Jan, the money's not in the bank. Far from it.' Nevertheless he reached for a crystal flute and filled it, 'Aren't you being a little premature?'

Jan's glance was sly. 'Not in the least, my friend. I have had a piece of news today which might interest you.' He waved a hand whose pudgy fingers sported several heavy gold rings, 'It concerns our plans for that land of yours.'

Roger stiffened. 'What news?'

'The first consignment of cannabis

68

seedlings is ready. It's on its way from Zululand, courtesy of my business partner. He is standing by to transport them by van tomorrow.'

Jan Theron lifted his glass and tossed back the pale gold liquid, some of which dribbled from the side of his mouth. Roger watched him with distaste.

'A large, ten-ton van.' Jan guffawed. 'A bakers' van, to be exact, hidden in a specially constructed compartment underneath all the cakes.' He laughed uproariously.

'Hang about,' Roger said in some alarm.

Jan's small eyes narrowed to slits. 'What do you mean?'

'I haven't secured the land yet, and then we will have to hire suitable labourers, men who will keep their mouths shut. I'm still working on it.'

Jan's bonhomie dropped off like rotten fruit from a tree. 'What do you mean, you haven't secured the land?' he thundered. 'You promised me, Roger, and on that basis I went ahead. What

69

are you playing at, man?'

'Yes, yes, I know I said you could proceed but I didn't realise everything would happen so quickly. There has been a slight hitch, that's all. I'll have it buttoned up soon, I promise. No need for panic.'

Jan scowled. 'You had better see that you deliver then, Roger,' he threatened, 'or things will not go well for you, old man. You know what happens to people who let me down.'

Roger did indeed know. Jan was a man of influence in the town and had a number of his fat fingers in a number of unsavoury pies. One word from Jan and he'd find himself blacklisted within days. As it was, his agency was not doing well and his credit rating had become decidedly shaky. The only reason his bank manager had advanced that last loan was that he'd hinted the family estate was soon to be his. Well, lied about it, actually, but what was a little deception between a man and his banker?

He practised it daily at work and his clients were none the worse for it. On the contrary, certain ones always seemed pleased at his wheeling and dealing on their behalf; even admired him for it. Jan Theron, however, was not a man to be lied to. He was a ruthless individual, not averse to organising some pretty unpleasant activities for those who crossed him.

Jan reached for another bottle of champagne and expertly popped the cork. 'I can put things off for a few days, Roger,' he growled, 'but not much longer.' He added with a threatening sneer, 'Close the door as you leave.'

Sulkily Roger thumped down his unfinished drink. He knew a marching order when he heard one and Jan Theron was not a man to be trifled with. He stood up, trying to look unconcerned. Hiding his fury, he said shortly, 'I'll be in touch.'

He stalked down the passage and slammed the front door. Damn Jasper once again! There was no more time to lose. He would have to work fast . . .

★ ★ ★

At five o'clock sharp Lexi locked her shop and carefully cashed up, pleased to see that the takings were higher than usual for a Tuesday. They'd had a busy day with busloads of tourists arriving to visit the town, keen to see its art gallery and the wine and brandy museum. They'd made a beeline for Gran's jams, too, especially the strawberry jam.

Her grandparents had cheered up considerably last night when she'd hurried from Maison Rousseau to tell them the good news about the lease. Gran, miraculously becoming her busy self once more, had immediately set about preparing the fruit for more jam, which was just as well. They were running out of stocks.

Lexi grinned as she swept the shop floor. 'At this rate we'll be rich in no time, and Gran's fame will spread far and wide.'

As usual she ensured that the kitchen was spotless and the tables were in readiness for the morning, with fresh flowers in the vases and clean cloths where needed. Before going up to her flat she went to find a plastic tub for Robbie's chocolate chip cookies.

What an endearing little boy he was — almost as endearing as his father. Not that she fancied the man or anything, what could be more foolish than that? She didn't go for married men even if their wives had left them because what would happen if said wives wanted to return? It was a total no-brainer and she, Lexi Smit, was one wised-up lady.

Upstairs in her small flat she took a quick shower and changed into a cool, ocean-coloured dress with thin shoulder straps and a wide skirt that swirled about her legs as she walked. It was one of her favourite outfits because it matched her eyes so exactly. At the last moment she decided to dispense with the heavy plait; it seemed rather unfriendly — not that she wanted to encourage Doctor Rousseau's friendship, exactly.

'I shall be polite and businesslike, and enjoy my meal,' she admonished herself firmly. 'That's all.'

She brushed out her silver-gold hair and secured it away from her cheeks with the silver combs which had once belonged to her mother. She treasured them because they were so daintily crafted, with tiny forget-me-nots in blue enamel which went perfectly with the studs in her ears.

Not a conceited girl, she was nevertheless pleased with her appearance.

'You're a credit to your Dutch heritage,' Grandpa would say, and Gran would agree, 'you're as pretty as a painted wagon, Lexi.'

And Doctor Rousseau, would he be impressed, too? Hastily she suppressed the small voice's query from her mind.

It had been extremely hot with a relentless sun beating down on the town. As Lexi parked her van an evening breeze rustled through the vines, cooling the grapes and allowing a respite from the heat. It also fanned her flushed cheeks and rustled her skirt as she walked across the flagstones to the front door. Glancing upwards she was once more deeply impressed by what was in effect a large Cape Dutch manor house.

Mrs Kama, watching from the window, had the door open before Lexi could lift her hand to the knocker.

'Good evening, Miss,' she beamed, and introduced herself with ill-concealed pride. 'My name is Maria Kama. I am the housekeeper, wife of Jakob the head gardener. Please come in.' Surreptitiously her eyes swept over Lexi's person from her tanned shoulders with their spaghetti straps to her high-heeled silver sandals from which peeped ten perfectly manicured, pearly-pink toes. Mrs Kama gave a sigh of pure pleasure.

She would inform Jakob later that evening that the young lady was very suitable to be the mistress of Maison Rousseau.

Ever since the previous evening she and Gerda had been laying bets in the kitchen that the master was in love with the cross lady in the blue van. He'd seemed very stern and thoughtful this morning, and had forgotten to sugar his porridge and then mislaid his car keys, but that was a good sign, was it not? It was time he took another wife but it must be a lady who knew how to cook his favourite dishes. Hadn't she informed Gerda that very morning that she, Maria Kama, was an excellent housekeeper? Yet she was bored with having to make meals that did not suit their native customs. Even Jakob disliked the master's European food.

Hearing voices, Robbie rushed downstairs, his small face alight with anticipation of his treat.

'Hello, Miss Smit,' he greeted her, his gaze already settled on the tub in her hand. 'Are those my cookies? Do they have chocolate chips in them? Did you make them all by yourself?'

Lexi smiled. 'They are indeed, Robbie, and yes, I made them this afternoon, like I promised.' She handed the tub over. 'Perhaps you could ask Mrs Kama to keep them in the kitchen until dinner is over.'

Mrs Kama approved greatly. She took the cookies to the kitchen and told an equally happy Gerda that they had indeed found the right lady for the master, for she would be able to please the menfolk with her food. She and Gerda would sample one of the cookies together right this minute, in fact, just to prove it.

'Miss Smit.' Jasper greeted his guest with an impassive face and a grave manner which belied the gleam of admiration in his eyes.

Lexi gave him a steady look, swallowing back a sudden rush of pleasure at the sight of him. The man was incredibly handsome, and his dark trousers and crisp shirt were not to be faulted. He seemed a little stern, which suited her fine. She disliked familiarity in a man, especially one she'd only just met; it made her want to flee like a scorched cat.

Her 'good evening Doctor Rousseau' was prim. She was determined she would not — but not — be impressed.

As though he knew what she'd been thinking, a sudden twinkle appeared. 'My name is Jasper. May I call you Alexandra?'

Lexi put her head on one side. 'Well, everyone calls me Lexi, it's less formal.' Then remembering her resolve to hold him at arm's length she said quickly, 'On second thoughts, Alexandra is fine.'

He hid a smile. 'No. Lexi it is, then.'

She stiffened. 'Very well Doct — em, Jasper.' As long as he wasn't about to ask her any personal questions or try to chat her up like that awful cousin of his, Roger, or whatever his name was.

To her astonishment Jasper did nothing of the sort. He seated her politely, offered her a glass of wine and sensing her reserve, set about giving her to understand she had nothing to fear. He carried on a matter-of-fact conversation about nothing much of great importance, allowing her time to feel at ease.

Lexi took stock of her surroundings with growing pleasure. The magnificence of the drawing room quite took her breath away with its crystal wall chandeliers and a gilt-decorated ceiling.

'I like your home,' she approved. There were numerous brocade chairs and sofas in muted pinks and faded golds, with scattered rugs on the yellowwood floor and a great, hooded fireplace for use on cold winter evenings. In one corner of the room was a large glass-fronted cabinet bearing items of silver and porcelain, obviously old and treasured.

By the time Mrs Kama came to announce that dinner was served Lexi felt as though she had known Jasper forever. As a result she became rather chatty, much to his secret amusement. Her eyes shone like diamonds and her pretty mouth curved most delightfully, causing his pulse rate, normally as steady as a ticking clock, to hasten into the fast lane. Hiding the chagrin he felt at his own susceptibility, he escorted her into the dining room.

Lexi's eyes widened at the sight of the enormous mahogany table. It had any number of matching ladder-back chairs upholstered in fine tapestry work which echoed the claret colour of the walls. The room was large, big enough for a banquet, and its walls were hung with several gilt framed paintings, and the finely crafted sideboard stretched almost from one end of the room to the other. It held an impressive variety of antique silver: candelabras, covered platters and a Georgian tea set her grandmother would have envied.

'I suppose they had big families in those days,' she remarked with not some little awe.

Jasper smiled mockingly. 'Do large

families frighten you, Lexi?'

'Of course not! When I marry I'd like at least five children. I'm an only child myself and it's been a little lonely at times. A house this size needs plenty of children, doesn't it?'

'Indeed it does,' Jasper agreed, knowing with an inner pang that Maison Rousseau would never see more than one while he was in residence.

Lexi was quick to see the pain in his eyes. Giving way to an unruly tongue she blurted warmly, 'Perhaps when your wife returns she would want to have more children . . . ' her voice tailed off uncertainly. He was looking as though he'd been concussed.

'I'm sorry,' she whispered, 'I had no right . . . please forgive me, it's none of my business.'

'No, it isn't,' he agreed calmly, thrusting aside the sudden, unaccountable wish that it was. He spoke with a gravity which belied his inner turmoil, but Lexi could see at once that he was annoyed, for his face was quite expressionless. For this reason she set out to make amends, becoming chattier as the meal progressed and revealing more of her own affairs than she would have wished. It was just as well she scarcely noticed the underdone potatoes, soggy vegetables and mediocre dessert.

'Papa,' Robbie whined, 'I don't want any more meat, I don't like it. It feels like elephant skin and the beans have feathers in them. Can I get my chocolate chip cookies, now?'

Jasper, who was struggling with his own tough steak and stringy beans, agreed. 'You may excuse yourself from the table, son, and say goodnight. Mrs Kama will take you upstairs and I'll be up shortly to hear your prayers.'

Robbie slid down from the table with alacrity. 'Excuse me, Papa, excuse me, Miss Smit.' At the door he came to an abrupt stop and turned and looked shyly at Lexi. 'Thank you for the cookies, Miss Smit.'

'You're welcome, Robbie.'

He hesitated. 'Miss Smit, will you come up and kiss me goodnight like Mama used to do?' He eyed her anxiously, 'Then maybe I won't have any bad dreams.'

Lexi shot an imploring look at Jasper. 'May I . . . ?'

His deep voice turned husky. 'You may do as you wish,' he said quietly.

For the rest of the evening Lexi sensed his withdrawal and secretly puzzled over it. If it hadn't been for the pain she'd glimpsed from time to time in those steely eyes she would have thought he was angry, and perhaps he was. It made her angry, too, on his behalf. In fact she worked herself into such a state that she became as cross as two sticks.

That wife of his must be crazy as a bed bug! Fancy abandoning a fine husband like Jasper and a wonderful son like Robbie — it beggared belief. The sooner the errant woman returned to her rightful place the sooner her poor husband's world would right itself. And she, Lexi Smit, could stop being foolish and put him right out of her head.

Jasper escorted her to the front door, secretly amused at her overt sympathy for his wife-less state. He listened patiently to her thanks, prettily uttered, and lifted one large hand to pat her absently on the shoulder. Whereupon Lexi, quite carried away by her feelings, leaned up and kissed him with considerable warmth. It was only when she heard his quick, surprised breath that she realised what she'd done.

'Goodnight, Jasper,' she muttered, and ran out into the darkness where she hoped rather desperately that the same breeze was still present to cool her flaming cheeks.

★   ★   ★

Leaving Jan Theron's imposing mansion Roger Rousseau climbed into his BMW and drove out of Stellenbosch to a settlement where he knew there were several unemployed young men who had worked for him before; men who would do anything for a quick buck. He rounded up half a dozen, issued their instructions and promised to be back after dark to collect them.

'We will need to make a number of visits to the dump,' he told them roughly, 'And it may take all night. Bring your own implements, spades, machetes and so on.'

Just before sunrise their task was completed and he drove them all home again, grinning like a mule that had just eaten a prickly pear cactus. He would establish an alibi by instructing his secretary to say they had been out of town overnight in case old Jasper suspected anything, and by tomorrow those two old bats would be ready to talk.

At eight-thirty Lexi, unlocking the door of The Old Brown Teapot to let Gina and Chantal inside, heard the telephone ringing in her flat.

'Come in, ladies,' she greeted them

before racing up the back stairs. It could only be her grandparents; everyone else had the shop's business number, and purposely so. She wished to keep the line free in case her grandparents ever needed her. It was odd. Gran never phoned this early unless something was wrong. Perhaps her last batch of jam hadn't turned out well and it wouldn't be ready as promised, in which case they would have to use the gooseberry jam instead.

'Hello?'

'Lexi,' her grandmother's voice came faintly down the line, 'Please can you come at once?' She gave a small catching sob. 'Something quite nasty has happened . . . '

6

Lexi raced downstairs, car keys in hand. 'Gina,' she called in a calm voice, 'Hold the fort for a while, will you? I'm going out to Sunnyfields for more strawberry jam. I'll be back as soon as I can.'

Gina nodded. 'Sure.' She scanned Lexi's face. 'Is there a problem?'

Lexi hesitated. 'My grandmother is worried about something. It's nothing which can't be sorted out, I'm sure. Will you ask Chantal to start on the scones in the mean time? There's more cream in the fridge.'

She smiled her thanks and walked composedly out of the shop. As soon as she was out of sight she raced around to the back of the building, fired Henrietta's engine and drove away from Stellenbosch as fast as she could.

Doctor Rousseau, who had just

dropped Robbie off at Mountain Monkeys Play School next door, paused for a moment to collect himself before entering The Old Brown Teapot.

Gina looked up in surprise. 'I'm afraid we are not open yet, sir.' She eyed him with interest. It wasn't often such an impressive male specimen dropped in for a cup of tea. It was such a pity he was too early, she would have liked to chat him up.

'No problem,' Jasper said politely. 'Is Miss Smit in?'

'Lexi? No, she was called away. Can I help you at all?'

Jasper produced the plastic tub. 'Be so kind as to give her this, with my thanks. The name is Rousseau. She, er, baked some cookies for my young son yesterday.'

Gina gave him a knowing look. 'Certainly, sir.' She viewed his departing back before hurrying into the kitchen. 'Chantal, did you hear that?'

'I did. Lexi's a dark horse, isn't she? Fancy keeping a man like that in her bag. Baking cookies for the son, indeed!'

Gina shot her a worried glance. 'You don't think she's involved with a married man, do you? If there's a son there must be a wife. He seemed rather disappointed that she wasn't here.'

Chantal shook her head. 'Not our Lexi, she has her head screwed on. No, he must be on his own; a widower or a divorcee or something.'

'I hope you're right. He's amazing. It will be interesting to see Lexi's reaction when we tell her he called.'

'And then we'll watch this space . . . ' They gave each other meaning smiles and went on with their tasks.

Lexi was at this moment racing up the drive to the cottage. Vaguely she registered that something wasn't quite right in her peripheral vision but she kept her foot on the accelerator without actually looking at the terraces, too intent on finding out what was bothering her grandmother. Perhaps the cooker had packed in, in which case she would have to raid her meagre savings to buy another one. Nothing must be allowed to interfere with Gran's work. It gave her too much pleasure.

She parked the van and flew indoors. 'What is it, Gran?'

Once more her grandparents sat glumly on the sofa, holding each other's hands in a tight clasp which only underlined their intense distress. On seeing her granddaughter, Mrs Smit burst into fresh tears.

'Did you see what they've done?' she sobbed.

Lexi put an arm around her grandmother's shaking shoulders. 'Who? What? What has happened?'

'Take a look out of the window,' her grandfather instructed, unable to hide his despair. 'We are finished, Lexi. It will take months to recover, if ever. We're too old . . . '

Lexi raced to the picture window and stared outside. The terraces, normally burgeoning with berries of every kind, were completely bare. Every last plant had been ripped from the ground, leaving only churned up earth where the birds were already pecking at the worms.

'Oh, heavens,' she whispered. 'What a mess.'

'Exactly. Someone has come during the night and destroyed our livelihood. There's not a bush or plant left standing. Every bit of fruit has vanished, doubtless to be sold on someone's stall in a market somewhere, or just dumped in the refuse,' her grandfather said. His breathing had become quite erratic.

'We could have borne the loss of the fruit,' her grandmother added, 'but they've left us with nothing. We have just walked around the entire property. If they'd only left the plants alive in the ground we could have started again, but everything's gone. Everything . . . ' she made an unsuccessful effort to control her sobs. 'Pulled up by the roots and carted away. It's a crying waste. Perhaps we should have listened to that man

91

and agreed to move out, then we wouldn't be in this mess. Now we shall have to move into an old age home.'

'There's no way we can start planting again,' her husband agreed sadly, 'We have no insurance and no capital. I'll have to start phoning around this afternoon for other accommodation . . .'

'Indeed you will not!'

An icy rage consumed Lexi so that her eyes blazed with indigo fire. 'You will do no such thing, Grandpa, do you hear? I'm going to contact the police this minute.' She stalked to the telephone and dialled the Stellenbosch Police Station, explaining the situation in a tight little voice which revealed nothing of the outraged tears she struggled to keep at bay.

Within half an hour two police officers arrived to examine the scene and take a statement. They appeared to be slightly indifferent until Lexi mentioned the name Rousseau, when Detective Inspector Shaw's head snapped up.

His gaze sharpened. 'This property belongs to the Rousseau family?' He scribbled a note on his pad. 'Mister Roger Rousseau?'

'I believe his name is Jasper — Doctor Jasper Rousseau,' Lexi informed him. 'He inherited the estate very recently.'

'I see. Would you mind starting at the beginning again, Miss . . . ?'

★   ★   ★

By the time the officers had left with the promise to look into things, Lexi had made two decisions. Whoever was responsible for this would be made to pay up, and on no account would she allow her grandparents to go into a home. It was heartbreaking, but if push came to shove she would be prepared to sell her business. They would use the proceeds to buy an inexpensive little house somewhere, preferably far away from the area with its memories of happier times, and make a new life for themselves.

It would not be easy to make ends meet but she had some small savings and perhaps she could get a bank loan to start another venture — a wool shop, perhaps. Gran was good with her knitting.

After making her grandparents a cup of coffee and ensuring her grandfather had his inhaler to hand Lexi went into the kitchen to start on the lunch. She had decided not to return to the shop. She would spend the rest of the day at the cottage since her grandparents were in no fit state to be left on their own.

When she telephoned the shop to explain that she would be returning too late to lock up and would one of the staff please do so and leave the cashing up for her later, she was informed by a curious Gina that the sexiest married man this side of Table Mountain had called to see her. A complete hunk, apparently, who could get any woman he liked on a slice of toast.

'What did he want?' Lexi asked,

without much interest.

'He wanted to return a tub,' Gina told her happily, 'A tub you'd given his son. Filled with cookies, I believe. He was all lathered up and mad as a red-eyed bull because you weren't in. My, but you're a dark horse, Lexi. Where did you find him?'

'Under a stone,' Lexi retorted crossly, 'Goodbye, Gina.'

She slammed down the phone and went icy cold as the hair began to prickle on the back of her neck, much like that on a fighting tomcat. Of course! Why hadn't she realized it before? The Rousseau's were responsible for this latest fiasco; it was blindingly obvious! Jasper and his odious cousin wanted her grandparents out of the way so they could get their fat hands on Sunnyfields Berry Farm. She'd been fobbed off very neatly by Jasper last night, and now he must be laughing in his boots.

Lexi took a deep breath and ground her teeth. To think she'd been such a great, gullible fool! And to think she'd actually felt sorry for him!

Without pausing for thought she informed her startled grandparents that she was going next door to demand an explanation from their stinking, treacherous neighbour. At the same time she was heard to mutter furiously about toads, bullfrogs and skunks.

'But Lexi, do you think that's a good idea?' her grandmother began, only to look helplessly at her husband, for Lexi was already racing down the drive in her blue van.

★   ★   ★

'What are you doing, locking the front door again? We've only just opened up.'

'We're going out for the day, Celine,' Roger Rousseau informed his secretary with a sly glance. 'In fact, we're staying overnight.'

He pocketed the keys and stroked her cheek with one large hand, the fingernails of which still sported traces of the soil he'd tried to remove that morning. He examined them in annoyance. It was a pity there was no time to book a proper manicure with that blonde bimbo on the other side of town who occasionally took care of his other needs.

Celine, another gormless female in Roger's patronising estimation, gazed at him adoringly. 'We are? Oh, Roger! Where are we going?' She ran her scarlet tipped hands over her perfect hairdo and appeared to gloat, just as though she thought her boss was about to appreciate her at last.

'I haven't decided yet, my little crocodile. But rest assured it will be well worth it. We'll shut up shop and simply disappear. I have a yen to indulge myself in a little holiday.' He winked suggestively, 'It's about time I rewarded you for all your hard work, angel. Don't bother about clothes, you won't need them,' he laughed as he ushered her quickly out of the back door.

Mrs Kama, busy sorting the linen, hastened to the front door to answer its thumping summons. She stared in consternation at the thunderous face before her. This time the young lady hadn't only swallowed a bee, she'd eaten a hornet as well. A wet one.

'Doctor Rousseau, please.'

'Doctor Rousseau is not here, Miss. He has gone up to the cellar to speak to the cellar master.'

'Where is this precious cellar?' Lexi snapped.

Mrs Kama pointed to the side of a mountain some way beyond the homestead. 'It's over there, Miss, just follow the path past the vines. The cellar is built right into the mountain for coolness, and you will have to go down the steps — ' she broke off as Lexi swung around and marched away at a furious pace.

Mrs Kama's brows drew together in a frown. Anyone could see the young lady was as mad as a teased cobra. She would go to the kitchen at once and ask Gerda what she thought about the situation. Maybe the young lady felt that the master was not taking enough notice of her. He was, after all, a very busy man.

Jasper, having discussed various matters with his cellar master, Marc Devine, was feeling satisfied with the man's judgement concerning the amount of yeast needed for the next vat. He was learning fast, having read most of the books on viticulture in his Uncle's library. His thoughts turned to the lecture he would attend the following week at the Winemaker's Guild; he mounted the steps from the cellar's cavernous interior and walked out into the sunlight.

It wasn't only the sudden light which caused him to blink. The woman who kept disturbing his thoughts was making like a steam engine up the slope and by the look of things he was about to receive another tongue-lashing. He grinned, wondering what kind of a circus it would be this time.

'There you are,' Lexi snarled.

Jasper's eyes twinkled. 'Good day, Lexi. To what do I owe this sudden pleasure? Or is it perhaps not a pleasure? You are angry enough to spit and unfortunately for me I'm standing well within your range. Let's hope that your aim is not very good.'

Lexi, already panting from her exertions, felt even more breathless at the sight of him. She ignored her traitorous emotions and said furiously, 'You odious beast! You will not fob me off this time. I want an explanation!'

'Beast?' he mocked, 'I thought I was toad. I do wish you'd make up your mind, Miss Smit.'

'I am waiting, Doctor Rousseau.'

'In that case, shall we go into the house? It's so undignified to be discussing our little contretemps in the open in front of the vineyard workers, don't you think?'

'No! You will tell me here and now

why you have seen fit to do what you've done — you and your lousy cousin; the one who has, quote, other uses for our land, unquote. I want an explanation, and I want it now.'

Jasper sighed, took her by the elbow and marched her down the path to the veranda. 'I haven't the least idea what you are referring to,' he said mildly. 'Shall we start at the beginning?'

'Certainly, if you want to play it that way. Get into my van,' Lexi ordered, 'and I'll drive you next door so that you may view your nocturnal handiwork in the light of day.'

Jasper raised his eyebrows. 'What handiwork? What do you mean?' His gaze locked with hers, suddenly intent. 'You're quite serious, aren't you? What is all this about?'

'Get in,' ordered Lexi.

'No.' He indicated a gate in the fence beyond the vines, one she'd had no idea even existed. 'Come along, it's quicker this way.'

Lexi followed him without a word

and then watched as Jasper stared uncomprehendingly at the churned up soil. He shrugged. 'So? You've had the bulldozers in.'

'No. *You've* had the bulldozers in! You did this during the night. I will be seeing my lawyer.'

'Whoa!' His startled grey eyes searched her face, 'Just a minute. You think that I had something to do with this? Why on earth would I wish to plough up your land?'

'I would have thought the answer to that is obvious: in order to force my grandparents out. Haven't you just devastated their livelihood with your wanton destruction of the whole orchard? Every last plant has been removed during the night, ripe berries and all. They are ruined.'

Jasper turned ashen. He let out a few choice words the like of which Lexi had never heard before.

Roger! This had to be his doing. He should have known his unscrupulous cousin would stop at nothing to get his own way. It was down to him now to do what he could to rectify the situation. And then he would get hold of the jerk and throttle him.

'Do you deny it?' Lexi demanded.

Jasper looked as though he didn't know where to start. 'What can I say?' he said heavily, 'Except that perhaps I should have foreseen something like this.'

'That's rich! I suppose you're going to say it wasn't you? Well, I don't believe you for a moment. You're a liar. You're both liars. Flaming liars.'

Sudden cold fury was etched on Jasper's face. 'Be quiet,' he rasped, and took her roughly by the arm. 'Come with me. I wish to speak to your grandparents.' Tight-lipped, he marched her down to the cottage.

Johannes and Marta Smit looked up in astonishment at the tall, grim-faced man who appeared suddenly in their living room with their granddaughter in tow. They listened wide-eyed to Jasper's deep voice as he offered a stiff but sincere apology for their misfortunes and declared himself ready to help them in any way he could.

'I realise you will have to replant the whole orchard and that it will be costly,' he finished. 'For this reason I intend to compensate you financially for your losses and will personally supply any extra labour you need to get the orchard up and running again as soon as possible. I can only say how deeply I regret that this has happened.'

They watched speechlessly as he reached into a pocket for his cheque book and mentioned a sum which made them gasp.

'But . . . ' began Mrs Smit, 'why should you feel that it is your responsibility to help us in this way?'

'Our troubles are hardly your concern,' Mr Smit agreed, adding 'We cannot accept your money, but we appreciate the kind thought.'

Jasper's eyes turned as dark as his troubled thoughts. 'I would be grateful if you could see your way to accepting my help, sir. Shall we just say that as your landlord I wish to make a gesture of goodwill?'

Mr Smit hesitated. 'Well . . . '

'We accept,' his wife intervened quickly, as pragmatic as ever. It would be foolish in the extreme to look such a wonderful gift horse in the mouth. 'How can we ever thank you? You have saved us from ruin.'

'Not at all. It is my land and I wish to see it in proper use.'

Jasper wrote quickly, tore out the cheque and handed it to Mr Smit. 'It's the least I can do, and please be assured I will get to the bottom of this unpleasant episode. Nothing like it must ever be allowed to happen again.'

Lexi, speechless, could only stare in bewilderment. Why was he doing this for them? Had she been horribly wrong in blaming him? Did he really have nothing at all to do with it? If so, why did he now feel the need to rescue them? It was as confusing as ever.

Jasper watched the bafflement in her eyes and the endearing tide of pink washing over her cheeks, and steeled himself to try to ignore both. He listened impassively as she added her thanks in a stiff little voice laced with utter confusion.

'It is most generous of you . . . '

Hiding a tender amusement, he gave her a long, hard look and conceded in a voice as cold as his wine cellar, 'No problem, Miss Smit. I trust you will now desist with all your petty and unfounded accusations. I find them insulting, to say the least.' He nodded to her grandparents. 'Good day to you. I'll see myself out.'

When he had gone the three of them viewed one another in stupefaction.

'What accusations?' her grandfather demanded.

'What have you done?' her grandmother whispered.

'Oh, sh-sh-shoot!' Lexi burst out angrily, narrowly avoiding the utterance of an unsavoury word which would have shocked her grandparents to the tips of their elderly toes. 'I called him a liar to his f-face . . . ' she stammered, and then she burst into tears.

7

Lexi awoke early, having spent a miserable night in the tiny spare bedroom of her grandparents' cottage. It was a short night of heavy sleep containing ridiculous dreams about toads in slimy ponds which hopped out and gobbled up all their berries. She grimaced as she dressed in yesterday's less than pristine skirt and blouse and dragged a brush through her long hair before tying it back with a ribbon.

'Not exactly your usual style, Lexi,' she muttered in distaste as she viewed herself in the mirror.

Hopefully nobody would be about when she went to retrieve Henrietta from Maison Rousseau. After that she'd drive to her flat for breakfast and a quick shower; then yesterday's takings still had to be dealt with before the staff arrived for work.

'Your breakfast, Gran,' she called as she tapped on the door of her grandparents' bedroom and entered with a tray of tea and toast.

Her grandmother was already awake and reading her Bible verses for the day. 'Thank you, dear. You're up early.'

'Yes. I must get back to Stellenbosch . . . the shop, you know.'

Mrs Smit noted the dark rings under her granddaughter's eyes and the decided droop to her pretty mouth. The dear child was still upset about last night. 'You didn't sleep well?' she enquired.

Lexi gave her a plastic smile. 'I'll be all right, Gran. I'm still a bit confused about everything. I mean, why did Doctor Rousseau give us that cheque if he didn't feel guilty about something? It doesn't quite add up. I still think he had something to do with it all.'

Her grandmother heaved herself on to one elbow. 'Lexi, my advice to you is to put it right out of your head, as your grandfather and I shall do. The good

Lord above has granted us a new start and we intend to get on with our lives without delay.'

'You're probably right, Gran.' But how could she just forget about it all?

During the small hours the shocking truth had hit her over the head with alarming force: she'd fallen for the wretched man like ripe plums from a tree, and that knowledge had kept her tossing about for the rest of the night.

In fact, her head was still buzzing. How could she have been so stupid?

'You will bank the money for us today, Lexi?'

'Yes, Gran, I will, as soon as the bank opens. I have the cheque safely in my handbag.'

Her grandfather turned over and coughed. 'Good morning, Lexi.' He looked altogether a different person; filled with new hope. 'It's going to be a wonderful day for us,' he remarked happily, 'Your grandmother and I will begin making plans about the orchard.' He turned to his wife. 'Shall we drive

110

out to that wholesale nursery near Franschhoek, my dear, and take a look at their catalogue?'

'Yes, Johannes, that is an excellent idea. We must obtain the very best strains this time. I believe their new lot of seedlings are almost ready.'

The old lady glanced at her grand-daughter. 'Was that not a generous gesture by our neighbour? It's the sort of thing old Jacques would have done, you know. I can see his nephew is a chip off the old block. A fine young man, do you not agree?'

Lexi muttered something inaudible.

'There is enough money,' her grand-father informed her, 'to tide us over until the new bushes start producing. In the meantime you will have to buy in the fruit for the jams. Will that be a problem?'

'No, Grandpa. I can go to the Farmer's Market.'

'Well, then. Have a good day, my dear.'

Lexi had never seen her grandparents

so happy and motivated. It was a pity she was unable to share their enthusiasm. She left the cottage and made her way through the gate Jasper had shown her the previous evening, trying to regain her usual bright spirits.

Just because she had fallen in love with the wrong man did not mean that her life had to come to a standstill. She must be sensible. After today she would keep well clear of Maison Rousseau and its enigmatic owner. She would keep very busy and continue to run her tea shop and be breathlessly efficient at it. There would be no time for romantic ideas about men, married or otherwise.

The blue van was still where she'd left it, parked outside the front door. Stealthily she crept across the gravel forecourt and paused to scrabble in her handbag for the keys, only to discover that they weren't there.

'Darn, darn, darn,' she grumbled, turning to search the ground nearby. She must have dropped them last night. She had to admit she'd been in rather a state so anything could have happened.

Jasper, watching her from his study window, permitted himself a small grin. For a large man he moved swiftly, letting himself silently out of the front door then walking towards her.

'Looking for these?' he asked blandly.

Lexi jumped. 'Don't you know you must never, ever creep up on people like that?' She glared at him fiercely in order to counteract the wild racing of her pulse, 'It could give someone a heart attack!'

He watched the pink wash over her cheeks and his eyes glimmered. 'I apologise. It was thoughtless of me.' He held out the keys, 'Yours, I think.'

Lexi snatched them much as a monkey would grab at a banana and swiftly unlocked the door of her car. She tossed him a cold glance. 'Goodbye, Doctor Rousseau.'

'Jasper,' he corrected.

She let off the handbrake, fumbled with the gears and fired the engine with such unnecessary force that Henrietta

113

gave a rather undignified jerk. A sweet smile curved her lips, completely at odds with the anger flashing in her blue eyes.

'That will not be necessary, will it? You and I will not be meeting again.'

Firmly she stamped on the accelerator and raced away, her pretty nose high in the air.

Jasper's wide shoulders shook with laughter. 'We'll see about that,' he grinned, and returned to the house.

★ ★ ★

Roger Rousseau decided to cut short his sudden 'holiday' because it was not turning out as he'd hoped. Celine bored him. She hadn't come up to his expectations at all. Every time he'd made an amorous advance she'd adroitly turned the conversation to her various hairstyles or her latest new outfit or her favourite soap opera. The crowning insult had been when he'd tried to take her to bed; she'd made some pathetic excuse about a migraine headache and demanded a room of her own.

'Her own room,' he muttered in disgust, 'I ask you!' Still, there were plenty of other fish in the sea. He'd book that manicure with the bimbo on the other side of town; she knew a thing or two about consoling a man . . .

Carelessly he slammed the door of his BMW and made his way around the side of the building to the office door. To his astonishment he discovered Jasper, standing there looking like thunder and holding up the doorpost with one large shoulder.

'A word with you, Roger.'

Roger smirked. It was just as he'd thought. Jasper had capitulated and was now ready to sign the lease.

'Certainly, cousin.'

He motioned Jasper into the office and stared at the sight that met him. Celine was already at her desk looking sleek and sexy in an off-the-shoulder sundress with glossy lipstick to match . . . Provocative Pink, he remembered she called it. Her wide, heavily made-up eyes and teasing blonde curls were as enticing as ever.

Roger ground his teeth. The woman was driving him mad but he'd treat her with contempt for a few days and she'd soon come running — that usually did the trick with women.

Celine rose obediently from the desk and fluttered about offering coffee, tossing her boss simpering looks from time to time and surreptitiously sizing up the visitor.

'You can stick your coffee,' Roger growled rudely, 'I'm busy.'

With a grimace Celine went to make her own coffee. The pig had got out of the wrong side of the pigsty this morning.

'See that I am not disturbed,' Roger ordered. He led Jasper to the back office and gave a nasty smile. 'To what do I owe this cousinly visit then, Jasper? Have you come to sign the lease for that land I want? I thought you'd see things my way — '

'Not at all,'' Jasper intervened silkily, 'I have no intention of allowing you even one inch of the estate.'

Roger eyed him with angry disbelief. 'What do you want, then? Like I said, I'm busy.'

'I want an explanation for the wanton destruction two nights ago of what is essentially still my property.'

Roger feigned astonishment. 'What do you mean?'

'Oh, you know exactly what I mean, cousin. Sunnyfields Berry Farm has been decimated.'

Roger played for time, stroking his stubbly, undershot jaw. 'You mean those two old bats? What happened, then? I have no idea what you are talking about.'

'It was an appalling piece of dirty work Roger, for which you are responsible. Don't bother to deny it.'

''Ah, but I do deny it. I have a suitable alibi so it couldn't have been me, could it? In actual fact I was taking a little break in Cape Town with my secretary. You can ask her to verify it. Celine,' he roared, 'come here.'

His secretary tottered into the room on her five-inch heels, obviously having eavesdropped just outside the door. 'Yes, Mister Rousseau?'

'Tell this gentleman where we were for the last two nights.'

Celine frowned. 'Two nights, Roger? It was only the one night, remember? We spent last night at Camps Bay in that fabulous hotel near the waterfront where they served the best oysters and champagne I have ever tasted. They gave me a splitting headache and I — ' she broke off at the thunderous look on her boss's face.

'It was two nights,' Roger grated, taking her by the arm in a bullying manner. 'Tell him, Celine, it was two nights.'

Celine looked confused. 'Was it? Oh dear, I'm not sure . . . '

'Stupid cow,' Roger muttered under his breath. Trust the woman not to back him up. He had a good mind to dismiss her.

'I think I get the picture, Roger,' Jasper told him blandly. 'Be assured that you will not get away with this. I advise you to stay away well from Maison Rousseau in future or you may find you have picked a fight with the wrong man.'

When he'd gone Roger sat down heavily and began to chew his nails. Old Jasper wasn't playing ball as easily as he'd hoped. Well, he had a few more tricks up his sleeve. As soon as he'd forced those old bats out of their home his cousin would have to co-operate. Surely the estate needed the rent money — perhaps he should offer to double it? He could always recoup the cash afterwards once they had sold the cannabis.

★   ★   ★

It was a few days later that Lexi looked up and saw Doctor Rousseau and his son enter The Old Brown Teapot. She was quite unable to hide her rush of delight, which she swiftly subdued, and greeted them in a voice as prim as a maiden aunt's.

Jasper, noting the reaction, allowed his unhurried gaze to sweep her suddenly pink cheeks. His eyes were very bright. He said softly, 'How beautiful you are, Lexi.'

Lexi's eyes blazed. She muttered something in Dutch, a language she seldom used. How dare he come on to her like that!

'What are you doing here?' she demanded, quite forgetting her usual polite manner.

Jasper's face became blank. 'Is that any way to treat a valued customer?' He added cooly, 'We have come for a cup of tea and more of those delicious cookies.'

'The ones with chocolate chips in them,' Robbie hastened to make clear. He added anxiously, 'Big cookies, please. Have you baked them today, Miss Smit?'

Lexi's hostile face underwent a miraculous change. She could never be unkind to a child. 'We have indeed, Robbie,' she smiled, 'Perhaps you would find a table and I'll ask Gina to take your order.'

'Oh, but surely you aren't too busy to take it yourself?' Robbie's father enquired silkily.

Lexi ignored him. She marched off to find Gina, who was only too willing.

'That gorgeous gent with the child? I'd love to go and chat him up.' She flicked back her long, dark hair and peered at him more closely. 'Oh!' she gasped, in sudden recognition, 'He's the hunk who fancies you, Lexi.'

'What rubbish,' Lexi snapped, and disappeared into the kitchen where she busied herself for the next hour until she was satisfied Jasper had left the shop. There was no way she was going to fraternise with him. There was still the matter of the destroyed orchard and, after all why would he have felt the need to compensate her grandparents for it if he hadn't been guilty?

Yes, she had foolishly allowed herself to fall for the man and yes, she wished more than ever that she could have him for herself and yes, she wished that he'd want her too. More than anything she wished that he'd want her. But she was a girl who had her principles and she stuck by them. The man was an enigma and until she'd unravelled the puzzle she would keep a tight rein on her emotions. She stared at Jasper's departing back feeling utterly frustrated.

The clock was striking six by the time she was ready to go up to her flat. She'd taken her time cashing up and making the dough for the pizzas; it would save them having to do it in the morning.

Thankfully she could now kick off her shoes and relax over a glass of wine. She intended to phone for a take-away meal from the curry house on the corner and afterwards watch her favourite television programme. Perhaps a quiet evening would restore her equilibrium. It had quite deserted her since setting eyes on Jasper Rousseau.

★ ★ ★

At that moment Jasper, having sent Robbie upstairs for his bath, was pouring his own glass of wine. He lowered himself into an armchair in the study and allowed his powerful brain to address the problem of Miss Alexandra Smit. She was one captivating lady who not only kept him awake at night, she also plagued his thoughts by day. It could not be allowed to continue; he had an estate to run.

His lips twisted wryly. 'Jasper, old boy, you surely know the signs! Despite your firm and oft-stated resolve not to allow another woman into your life, you are deeply smitten.'

He gave a frustrated sigh as he tried to understand what made her tick. Lexi was warm and feminine at one moment and a fierce, spitting kitten the next.

She would be resolutely prim and then happily chatty; a disconcerting combination. Yet she was quite unable to hide her fierce loyalties and her endearing naivety. She would make an interesting wife . . .

8

Early the following morning Lexi drove to the Farmers' Market near the Eikestad Mall to purchase the strawberries for her grandmother's next batch of jam. As she parked the van she noticed two young women seated near the roadside selling a variety of berries from a stall. It was not unusual to find people hawking their goods in this manner and she approached them, thinking she might find a few bargains.

'Good morning. Do you have any strawberries?'

The women gave each other a meaningful look. The one in the red scarf giggled. 'The strawberries got crushed, like. The men were not very careful with them. No, Miss, there are no strawberries.'

'But we have other berries, nice and fresh, Miss, and very cheap,' the other said, pointing to a number of plastic bags already filled with ripe raspberries and gooseberries.

They both looked rather down-at-heel in their shabby dresses and headscarves, so Lexi, ready to be kind, decided to support their venture by buying a number of the bags. The berries were always carefully washed before use, anyway.

'Will you be here next week?' she asked. 'I would like to buy some of your strawberries then, if you have any.'

The woman giggled again. 'No Miss, we will not be here. We got these berries yesterday, one lot only and there will be no more next week. We got them — ' She clapped a hand over her mouth as though she'd said too much.

'From the dump,' supplied the other woman naively.

'Shut your big mouth, Katrina,' her friend rounded on her, 'You are not supposed to say that.'

Lexi went very still. 'The dump? You mean you found all these berries on a dump? Which dump? When exactly was this?'

The first woman looked sulky. 'They were thrown away and my boyfriend told me to pick them. He said we should take the berries off the bushes and sell them. We haven't done anything wrong.'

'No,' Lexi said thoughtfully, 'I don't suppose you have. Were there a lot of bushes on the dump?'

The woman, however, wasn't saying anything further. 'I don't know,' she said sullenly.

Lexi smiled brightly as she handed over some notes. 'Keep the change. I'm sorry you won't be here next week. Goodbye.'

Clutching her purchases she returned to the van. If what she suspected was true then those berries had come from Sunnyfields and Detective Inspector Shaw needed to know about them. She would drive to the police station at once.

D.I. Shaw listened intently. 'Near the

Eikestad Mall, you say? I'll send someone to bring them in for questioning. Thank you for the information, Miss Smit.'

'Of course, I may be quite wrong.'

'Indeed.'

'The women were only trying to make a little money,' she reminded him.

He gave her a fatherly smile. 'Don't worry, Miss Smit. Justice will be done in the end, one way or another.'

* * *

Roger Rousseau was in a bad mood. He had one day in which to act and he needed to think of something, fast. Jan Theron had just telephoned to inform him that the seedlings were on their way. In fact, they were at this moment not very far from Cape Town. The baker's van would park in a lay-by overnight and when it arrived in Stellenbosch in the morning it would stop outside Mountain Estates for further instructions. It was to be hoped that he, Roger, would not fail at this late stage or he, Jan, would be forced to take certain other measures.

Roger sat at his desk and chewed his nails, watched surreptitiously by a curious Celine. Something was eating the boss and she knew exactly what it was, having listened in on the conversation only moments before. Something about a van full of cakes. She went to the ladies' toilet and made a swift call on her cell phone. Then well satisfied, she smiled at herself in the mirror and returned to the office to offer her boss a nice cup of tea.

Roger declined rather rudely. 'I am going out, Celine,' he told her shortly, 'Hold any further calls until I get back, and don't sit on your backside while I'm out, do you hear?'

'Yes Roger, no, Roger,' she chanted, poking unconcernedly at her blonde curls. 'Where will you be, in case I need to contact you?'

'You need to know nothing, Celine.

Just keep out of my business,' he snapped, and hurried out.

Calmly his secretary watched him go. When she was certain the BMW was out of sight she rose from her desk and began to rifle through certain papers, pausing now and then to use the photocopying machine. Her boss, she reflected in disgust, was the most stupid man she'd ever met.

Once more Roger drove to the settlement on the outskirts of town and recruited two young men whom he knew to be reliable.

'I have another job for you,' he told them. After giving them their instructions he produced a wad of notes. 'I want the place burned to the ground,' he ordered. 'I'll pick you up at ten o'clock tonight. See that you have enough petrol and lighters. You can make your own way home. I will be nowhere near the scene, you understand? You can collect the rest of your money when the job's done to my satisfaction.'

He turned away, failing to notice the ragged old man dozing nearby, apparently uninterested in what went on around him. Once the BMW was out of sight the old man sprinted to a blue sedan parked down the road and climbed inside.

'Get going,' he told the other plain clothes officer, 'We're on to something definite at last.'

* * *

Lexi cashed up as usual and locked the shop after Gina and Chantal had left. The two of them had been casting concerned glances at her all afternoon, convinced that she was sickening for something. Their employer's usual good nature appeared to have deserted her. Gina had mislaid a pizza pan and Chantal had burnt the last batch of scones and Lexi, normally so relaxed about these slight mishaps, had all but snapped their heads off.

It was Friday evening and as she took

herself up the back stairs Lexi envisioned a long evening ahead with nothing to do but sit in her flat and mope. She'd never felt so low; not since that awful black despair when her beloved parents had been killed. It was an uncomfortable experience for someone who had purposely developed a happy, upbeat personality; possibly as an armour against life's further blows.

Much as she'd tried, she could not dismiss Jasper Rousseau from her mind and it was causing her more pain as the days went by, not less. Her instincts told her he was a man of integrity and yet her mind still doubted him. If only she could be sure!

On a sudden impulse she decided to spend the weekend at Sunnyfields with her grandparents. It was no good having an evening out with any of her friends because she would not be very good company. They would demand to know what was wrong and she had no intention of telling them. Besides, Gran and Grandpa would be happily full of their plans for the new orchard; it would help to take her mind off her own anguish. Not even to herself did Lexi admit that she hoped for a glimpse of their next door neighbour . . .

At ten o'clock her grandmother yawned. 'I'll go to bed now, I think. Are you coming, Johannes? It's been a busy day for your grandfather and me, Lexi. Perhaps you wish to turn in, too?'

Lexi quickly agreed. The sooner the day ended the better, as far as she was concerned. It hadn't been a happy one.

⋆　⋆　⋆

An hour later young Robbie, waking from a heavy sleep, gave a piercing cry. 'Papa, Papa!'

Jasper, who had been pacing his study in exasperation as he tried to decide what to do about Lexi, raced upstairs to the bedroom.

'What is it, Robbie?'

'I had a bad dream again, Papa,' the child sobbed.

133

'I'm sorry to hear it, old man.' Jasper sat on the bed and placed an arm about his son's shoulders, holding him for a moment against his chest. 'Will a mug of cocoa and a cookie make you feel any better?'

'I think so, Papa.'

As Jasper stood up to go he noticed that Robbie's curtains were not properly closed and went to draw them. What he saw outside caused him to utter a startled gasp.

'What the . . . ?'

A sheet of fire had engulfed the outbuildings next door and was rapidly spreading to the Smit's cottage.

'Robbie,'' Jasper said in a calm voice, 'Be a good boy and read your Noddy book while I'm gone. I may be a little while getting those cookies . . . '

Satisfied that the child had his two teddy bears nearby for comfort he raced down the stairs to the telephone in the hall. A few seconds later he was running through the vines towards the gate, only to pause in horror when he saw the flames beginning to lick at the thatched roof.

Without thought for his own safety he charged repeatedly at the door with his shoulder, ignoring the burning pain it caused him. Eventually the door gave way, crumbling into charred remains at his feet. Shoving his handkerchief over his mouth and nose, he plunged into the smoke and fought his way to the bedroom area.

Within seconds he had woken the old couple who, dazed and frightened, allowed themselves to be escorted outside to the yard where they stared in speechless stupefaction as they watched their home burn.

'Lexi,' Mrs Smit moaned suddenly, 'Lexi's still inside . . . '

With an oath Jasper leapt resolutely back into the flames, careless of his burnt hands. He located Lexi at once, asleep under the duvet and still blissfully unaware. It was only as he dragged her from the bed and hefted her on to a painful shoulder that she awoke.

'Jasper,' she murmured groggily, 'What are you doing? I was just dreaming about you . . . '

'It's all right, my love,' he gasped.

Once outside she came fully awake and gave a choked scream, coughing and gasping as her stinging, horrified eyes took in the scene around her. Jasper, gasping for breath himself, placed an arm about her shoulders as the sound of a fire engine screamed through the night. Behind it could be heard more sirens, this time belonging to the police cars.

It was a glum little party who made its way some time later to Maison Rousseau. Mr and Mrs Smit and Lexi, shivering in their nightwear, were given blankets to shroud themselves while Jasper went to wake Mrs Kama and organise hot drinks.

Detective Inspector Shaw and his men had long since returned to Stellenbosch, having apprehended the two culprits as they fled along the road. All the men involved in the previous episode had also been rounded up during the evening, thanks to information supplied by the two women at the stall. The men would be questioned first thing in the morning, the Inspector had informed them, adding confidently that it wouldn't be long before the whole truth were known.

Mrs Kama, entering Tante Magda's small sitting room with a tray, showed suitable dismay. For once she was without words and stared at them with sorrowful brown eyes. When they viewed Lexi's smoke-blackened face, she could contain herself no longer.

'Oh, Miss,' she wailed, 'Please do not be cross with the master, he is a very wonderful man.'

Much to her amazement, Lexi found herself agreeing. 'Yes. Yes, he is,' she acknowledged in a wobbly voice, 'He saved our lives . . . ' and trailed off with a great sniff.

Without giving further thought to his own injuries Jasper took charge of the situation. 'You will all remain here tonight,' he told them firmly, 'I have just telephoned Doctor Mackenzie, who will see to any medical needs; he should be here shortly. My housekeeper is preparing the guest bedrooms and she will you show you to them shortly.'

He noted in some concern that the old man was having considerable difficulty with his breathing, and Mrs Smit looked as though she could do with a sedative. She was still sobbing quietly, clutched tightly in her shocked husband's embrace.

As soon as the doctor had departed, having left additional medication for Mr Smit, treated the old people for shock and dressed Jasper's burns, Lexi found her voice. 'We would like to s-say how grateful we are for all your help,' she gulped.

'What help?' Jasper's voice held a harsh, grating note. He was pale beneath his tan and looked more grim than a granite slab in a graveyard.

'It's the least I can do. This is entirely the fault of my own damned family.'

Lexi's lovely, tired eyes opened wide, framed by their thick sweep of dark lashes. Her mouth dropped open. She blinked and closed it with a snap, quite unable to think of anything further to say.

'May we go up to bed now?' asked Mrs Smit in a quavering voice. She looked about to collapse.

Jasper sprang up. 'Of course, my dear.' He stretched out a long arm and helped her gently to her feet just as Mrs Kama appeared to escort them up the stairs. 'I trust you will be comfortable,' he said bleakly, 'Please treat this as your home and ask for anything else you may need.'

They were half way up the wide staircase when a small voice was heard to wail plaintively, 'Papa, where are you?' The voice became cross. 'I'm still waiting for my cocoa and cookies . . . '

9

Early on Saturday morning Roger Rousseau stalked into the inner office and slammed the door. He picked up the telephone and dialled Jan Theron's number, waiting impatiently until he heard the man's voice.

'Look, Jan, you will have to give me a little more time,' he said firmly, hiding his fear. 'I will be signing the lease for that land today and when the present occupants have left the property, which should happen by this afternoon unless they, er, have expired in the night,' he joked slyly. 'We need to instruct the baker's van where to go. It's standing outside my office right this minute and I cannot allow it to remain there. It's dangerous — too conspicuous. We don't want any traffic police nosing around.'

Jan Theron, having had his breakfast

140

interrupted, swore roundly. 'You had better tell the driver to come here, then, Roger. Get in that fancy car of yours this minute and guide him here but take a roundabout route, understand? He can park behind my house for the next few hours. I will speak to you later.'

Relieved, Roger slammed down the phone. So far, so good.

By midday he began to feel uneasy. He'd parked the van as instructed but he hadn't heard from Jan again; the man had promised to be in touch, and to crown it all Celine hadn't arrived for work so he'd been forced to brew his own tea. He'd heard not a word about the fire from the two men he'd hired, but no doubt they would soon be turning up for their money.

He sat and gnawed at his fingernails, telling himself that he'd give it another half hour and then drive out to Maison Rousseau with the lease agreement. Jasper would be only too happy to sign it now.

At that moment his secretary marched through the door.

'Sorry I'm late, Mister Rousseau,' she said breezily, 'But I had some important business to see to.'

Roger gave her a furious look. 'I do not employ you to take time off without my say-so,' he replied sourly, 'You're fired.'

She smiled sweetly at him. 'In that case you won't mind if I make my friend a cup of coffee before I go?' She stood aside to allow a tall gentleman in a dark suit to enter the room and added, 'Meet my friend, Detective Inspector Shaw.'

Roger's head snapped up in alarm. 'What?'

'Roger Anthony Rousseau?'

'Yes. What the heck do you want? I suppose you're Celine's latest boy-friend? No wonder she wouldn't allow me near her the other night. Well, you can just push off . . . ' he trailed off suspiciously and looked from one to the other with growing unease.

'You are under arrest.' The Inspector turned to Celine, whose mouth was stretched in a wide smile. 'Cuff him, Sergeant,' he instructed.

'With the greatest of pleasure,' purred Detective Sergeant Celine Retief (Plain Clothes Division). She kicked off her five inch heels and lunged at her 'boss'. Roger, a heavy man, nevertheless found to his great astonishment that within seconds he was lying on his stomach on the floor.

'Hey, you can't do this!' he blustered. 'I'm innocent! What have I done?'

Inspector Shaw gave it to him straight. 'Fraud on twenty-two counts, money laundering, malicious and wanton destruction of property, arson with attempted murder, intention with co-accused to propagate an illegal substance, enticement to commit theft . . . ' The list went on.

The look on Roger Rousseau's face was to die for, Sergeant Retief later informed her colleagues. It quite made up for all those tedious months of under-cover investigation when she'd been forced to endure the man's uncouth manner, bloated ego and revolting, amorous advances. Besides, she'd found it very insulting to be labelled a bimbo; she, who had an honours degree from Stellenbosch University.

However, the hours she'd spent taping Roger's conversations and reproducing incriminating evidence had been well rewarded. There was enough evidence for convictions which would put him away for a long time to come — together with his buddy, Jan Theron.

As with all bullies, Roger was a coward. As he was led away to the police car he was heard to whine, 'It's not my fault. It's Jasper's . . . ' after which his snarls could be heard all the way down the street.

*　*　*

Sorrowfully Lexi stared out of the window at the smoking remains of

Sunnyfields Berry Farm. Both her grandfather's elderly red Toyota and her own dear Henrietta were ruined, burnt-out shells. She returned to the dressing table and combed her fingers through her hair in an effort to restore some order, then padded barefoot downstairs in her pyjamas.

Despite having made liberal use of the toiletries she'd found in one of the bathrooms, she still smelled of smoke. All she wanted now was to go home, take a shower and wash her hair. After that she would throw her singed pyjamas into the trash.

Her grandparents were still asleep and she was unwilling to disturb them. She made her way quietly to the dining room where Jasper, eating his breakfast with Robbie, rose from the dining table at the sound of her voice and surveyed her from head to foot. Even in her bedraggled state he found her to be incredibly lovely.

Lexi's greeting was curt; her eyes wary. He may have saved her life but it was nevertheless galling to feel so indebted, especially when he'd said with his own mouth that the Rousseau family were responsible for all their woes. She still could not understand it all.

'Good morning Lexi. 'Help yourself to anything you like. Bacon and eggs, toast, coffee ... they're all on the sideboard. I trust you slept well?''

When she informed him in a stiff little voice that she had slept as well as could be expected under the circumstances, he gave an inner sigh.

'Lexi my dear,' he advised her gently, 'I suggest you drop your guard. I have no wish to jump your bones this early in the morning, nor do I intend to devour you on my wholemeal toast.' He watched her cheeks redden and continued, 'Can we not be friends, at least?'

Lexi gulped. She met his steady grey eyes and her heart began to bounce against her ribs. She ignored it and said firmly in an even little voice she was proud of, 'I am not ungrateful for all you have done for us, Jasper, but you and I can never just be friends.'

How could she only be a friend when all she really wanted was to be his wife? She wanted to fling herself against that broad chest and tell him she'd love him forever even if he was a scoundrel; but it would be an unspeakably foolish thing to do.

Hadn't she just poked about in the wardrobe of her room and seen a woman's navy jogging suit hanging there, one with a bright pink trim and matching trainers? And what about that expensive make-up in the drawers of the dressing table, along with the black negligee?

Jasper gave her a long look which hid his feelings. 'In that case,' he remarked blandly, 'Can I offer you another cup of coffee?'

★ ★ ★

It was Sunday afternoon. Jasper had very kindly driven them to Lexi's flat in his Mercedes and after she had taken a shower she nipped along to the large chain store on the corner to purchase a variety of garments and some slippers which she deemed suitable for her grandparents to wear in the meantime. As soon as they had recovered a little more she would take them into town for a proper shopping spree. They would need new shoes and spectacles, for a start.

Lexi carried a tray of tea into her small living room and said firmly, 'Gran and Grandpa, I should like to run one or two ideas by you.'

Her grandmother sighed. 'Yes, Lexi. I daresay we need to decide what is to be done now.'

'I can't say I have much enthusiasm for anything,' her grandfather added. He looked quite ill, his face as grey as a wet Monday.

'We have all had a great shock,' Lexi agreed in a kind voice, 'But we are Smits and we will survive; it's what our family has always done, ever since arriving in this country in the seventeenth century.'

She smiled at them. 'Now this is what I propose to do . . . ' and she told them everything she had been thinking about.

'Are you sure you want to sell your business?' her grandmother asked, greatly concerned. 'What will you do afterwards?'

'I have a little money to tide us over.'

'You may use our small savings, too, Lexi,' her grandfather offered without hesitation. He added thoughtfully, 'Naturally we will return that money to Jasper Rousseau. There is now no need to re-establish the orchard, is there? We shall not be returning to Sunnyfields. Will you use an estate agent to advertise the business?'

'Not at first. I'll offer it privately to Gina and Chantal. They mentioned some time ago that they intended to start up on their own one day and I feel sure they could get a bank loan because Gina's father is the lending officer at Barclays. One of them could take over the flat when we move out.'

'Where will you live?' asked her

grandfather. 'Naturally your grand-mother and I will go to a home so as not to be a burden to you.'

Lexi shook her head. 'No. I intend to look after you for as long as it takes and that is not negotiable, Grandpa. I shall find another job and we will buy a small house somewhere with the proceeds of the business; if necessary I can apply for a small mortgage. We will move away from Stellenbosch, right away — I couldn't bear to continue living here, especially now that . . . ' she broke off with a sudden sob.

'Especially now that . . . ?' asked her grandmother.

'Well, just everything that's happened.' How could she tell her grandparent that she couldn't bear to be anywhere near Maison Rousseau because she had fallen in love with its owner?

He might well be a good man but he belonged to a very strange family who went about destroying people's lives. And what about that absent wife of his? Her clothes were still in that cupboard.

Lexi gulped the rest of her tea and smiled brightly to hide her pain.

'This is what I suggest. I'll phone Gina tonight and if she's interested I'll advise her to see my accountant, Mister Gerard, for any information the bank may require. Then I'll phone my friends Tom and Lucy, who can lend us their holiday cottage on the west coast at Paternoster. I've been there before and it is just what we need right now. The beaches,' she enthused, 'are glorious — absolutely wild and completely isolated; you can see for miles. It's a beautiful little fishing village with one or two shops and a hotel; just the thing to allow us to catch our breath and recover. What do you think about a fortnight's holiday in the fresh air?'

★ ★ ★

A week later, once the burns on his shoulder and hands had healed some-what, Jasper drove into Stellenbosch to

151

collect his son from Mountain Monkeys Play School. It was twelve thirty and after a busy morning supervising the vineyard workers in their spraying operations, he wanted a cup of tea. En route, however, he stopped to buy a large floral arrangement in the hope that it would provide the Smits with a little cheer.

He took Robbie by the hand and entered The Old Brown Teapot where he placed the basket of roses with its card on the counter. Then he made for their usual table near the window. The shop was full and the two waitresses busily at work but Lexi was nowhere to be seen.

Gina, her sharp eyes gleaming, descended on him with a bright smile. It was Lexi's heart-throb again, looking like the gorgeous hunk that he was.

'Good afternoon, sir. Is it to be tea and chocolate chip cookies again?' she asked, having remembered their order from the previous time.

Jasper thanked her politely and

enquired in a casual manner, 'Is Miss Smit here?'

Gina grinned knowingly. 'Oh, no, sir. She's gone.'

Jasper's eyebrows rose. 'Gone? Where?'

'She's taken her grandparents away. You are looking,' she informed him proudly, 'at the new owner of The Old Brown Teapot. At least, I will be shortly — I'm in the process of buying the business from her.'

Jasper's eyes narrowed. 'I see. Would you mind telling me where the Smits have gone to?'

'Paternoster, I think.'

'Good grief.' That was miles away on the west coast.

Gina, who read a great many romances, loved to stir matters once in a while. She gave Jasper a meaningful look. 'It's my belief that Lexi is unhappy in love, sir. That's why she has gone away. Well, she had to, hadn't she? She's in love with a married man and that would never do.'

Jasper went very still. 'Explain that remark.'

'Well, anyone can see that you're married, what with a little boy and all . . . ' she broke off, conscious that she may have said too much. 'I'll fetch your order, sir,' she added hastily, and fled to the kitchen.

Jasper sat staring at the table cloth until Robbie pointed out in an aggrieved little voice that his tea was getting cold, whereupon he stirred himself and shook his head to clear it. It couldn't be true. Lexi in love with him? And she still thought he was married! It explained a lot.

Sudden elation filled him.

He would make arrangements for his sister to take care of Robbie and leave the vineyard in the care of his cellar master for a few days. He would drive up the coast to Paternoster and knock on every door until he found her. It was high time he discovered what really made Lexi Smit tick.

* ★ ★

After a few hours watching the fisherman bring in their catches Lexi went into the tiny village store to purchase one or two newspapers for her grandparents to read during the afternoon. She glanced at one of the headlines and froze. Something about Roger Rousseau. She hurried back to the cottage to read it.

'Oh, my great, sainted aunt,' she gulped.

'What is it, love?' her grandmother asked. Sitting in an armchair with her newly purchased wool, she was casting on the stitches for a blue sweater for Johannes. She intended to finish it in time for Christmas, which was just around the corner.

'It says here that Roger Rousseau — you remember, that nasty man who visited you and tried to get you to leave Sunnyfields? Well, he has been charged with arson and fraud and a number of other offences.'

155

'I knew he couldn't be trusted! It was those eyes.'

'And it was he who burnt down the cottage and ruined the orchard.'

'What?' Mrs Smit looked shocked.

'It says here that he paid some young men from the settlement to do the dirty work for him.'

Her grandfather looked up from his crossword puzzle. 'But why on earth would he do that?'

'Well, I see it all now,' Lexi said slowly, 'Roger really did want that land for his own purposes, whatever they were, and he tried to get it by forcing you and Gran out.' She tossed the newspaper down. 'Jasper was right when he said his family were responsible for our troubles.'

'But not Jasper himself.'

'No, not Jasper himself.' Lexi rose from the sofa. She had been a great fool and she was ashamed she'd ever doubted him. But it was too late now.

'I think I'll go for a walk along the beach, folks. I'll be back in an hour to make your tea.' She needed time to process her thoughts.

It was quite a readjustment to realize that Jasper was not as black as she had been determined to paint him. If only he wasn't married, she'd go and look him up and say she'd changed her mind; they could still be friends — and who knew where that would lead?

Great tears rolled down her cheeks as she trudged along the sand, uncaring of the icy Atlantic waves on the shoreline which washed over her sandaled feet and soaked the edges of her denim jeans.

The wind had increased in the last few minutes, whipping her long hair about her head like a bright banner. The sky had changed, too. It was just two o'clock in the afternoon and yet it was becoming dark, with ponderous clouds building up over the sea. It would rain soon; great, icy drops lashing the landscape.

Although the beach was deserted, a masculine bellow alerted Lexi to the fact that she was not alone. She turned around, peered at the newcomer and froze.

Jasper stood before her, large and calm and very assured, with his dark hair flying untidily in the wind and his grey eyes fixed intently on her face. Unable to do more than gape, Lexi was filled with a delight she found quite impossible to hide.

'Wh-what are you doing here, Jasper?'

'Looking for you, Lexi.'

Jasper put his hands very firmly into his trouser pockets in order to keep them from reaching for her. It would not do to kiss her just yet. He first had to find out what she wanted.

'Why?' she asked baldly. 'Why have you come all this way?'

He took her by the arm and turned her around. 'Shall we go home? This weather is becoming unpleasant and I can hardly hear you speak.'

'Home?' Lexi cried wildly, 'I haven't a home, you should know that!'

Suddenly all the tensions of the previous week overcame her. She would soon be jobless and she would have to provide for the three of them, and Christmas was coming and they had very little money and where were they to live . . . ? Beside herself, Lexi began to sob.

'Lexi, Lexi my love,' Jasper soothed. He drew her against his chest and held her for as long as it took to sob out her anger and fright. Then he cupped her face with his hands and allowed her to see deep into his slate-grey eyes. But what she saw there only caused a fresh outburst of tears.

'No, Jasper,' she sobbed, 'You must not tell me that you love me. You're a m-married man.'

'No I'm not.' He kissed her, gently at first and then with fierce hunger. It was something he'd wanted to do for days. 'How many times must I say it, Lexi? I have no wife. She died in an accident.' Time enough when he would tell her all the sordid details, but not now. Now was the time to reassure her with his love. But he would need to go gently.

Lexi lifted her head. There was something she still needed to know. 'What about those clothes in the wardrobe?'

He frowned. 'What clothes? It is quite usual, my dear Lexi, to keep clothes in a wardrobe.'

'They were a woman's clothes . . . a navy jogging suit and pink trainers and a black negligee . . . designer make-up and two gorgeous bottles of perfume . . . ' she broke off at the look on Jasper's face. His great shoulders were shaking with laughter. 'What are you laughing at? If you have no wife then who do those things belong to?'

If he admitted he had a mistress she knew her heart would break into even smaller pieces.

'My younger sister, dear girl. Therese is at university in Cape Town and often comes to stay with me for the weekend, especially when she's between boyfriends, which happens with monotonous regularity. Satisfied? So you see, my darling Lexi, you have nothing to fear. I do not go in for casual liaisons.'

'No,' she gulped. 'I've been rather stupid.'

'Indeed you have,' Jasper agreed. He kissed her again with such tenderness it took her breath away. Gently wiping the last of her tears with his handkerchief, he was moved to tell her yet again how beautiful she was. This time Lexi gave a shuddering sigh and said earnestly, 'I don't usually cry much, you know. I'm generally a very happy person but I've been so unhappy recently . . . '

'I know.' He grinned, 'Your friend Gina was at pains to inform me that you were crossed in love.'

Lexi giggled. 'The rat.'

'She also revealed that she was about to purchase The Old Brown Teapot from you.'

'Yes, that's correct.'

She said it with such great sadness

that Jasper folded his large arms around her in a bear hug. He kissed her on the cheek this time, a gentle, caring salute. But when Lexi turned her face and began to kiss him back, he knew he had to call a halt.

When he had his breathing back under control he announced, 'I have some news for you, Lexi, and I hope it will cause your delicious, pearly-pink toes to curl up in delight. It may even be some small compensation for all the trouble Roger has caused, but we'll go home first and discuss it with your grandparents.'

Meekly Lexi agreed. Whatever it was that dear, generous, reliable Jasper had up his sleeve, she would never doubt him again.

By this time great drops of rain began to descend upon the beach. A bird, flapping its wings fiercely in the wind, skimmed over Jasper's head.

'Mind that seagull,' Lexi cried in alarm.

'That's not a gull, it's a Cape

Gannet,' Jasper corrected with a good-humoured laugh, and, because he liked to make things quite clear, murmured, 'Morus capensis.'

Lexi wasn't interested in gulls and gannets. All she wanted at that moment was to avoid the rain. 'Race you to the road,' she challenged, and flew ahead like an arrow. Jasper, admiring her from behind and conscious of a great feeling of relief, breathed a happy sigh.

10

Christmas came and went. It was six weeks later and the papers were signed. Gina and Chantal were now the proud co-owners of The Old Brown Teapot. The floor space came complete with all the kitchen appliances together with the small flat above, which the girls would share while they worked to ensure that the business continued to profit under their direction. It had a good name and they were sure that their many customers would continue to support them, but one thing would be sorely missed: Mrs Smit's jams and relishes.

'Never mind,' Gina told her friend brightly, 'We mustn't be ungenerous. We'll send a card to wish them well in their new venture, and continue to buy in our jams from the wholesaler.'

'Yes,' Chantal agreed, 'In time the customers will stop asking for Mrs

Smit's jars and simply enjoy what we have to offer.'

'Right, then. Let's get on with the baking. Lexi will be moving out in two days' time so we'll have plenty of opportunity over the weekend to redecorate the flat. She said she'd leave all her furniture for us as they will be buying everything new. Aren't they lucky?'

★ ★ ★

Lexi was at that moment in seventh heaven, choosing curtains and carpets in Cape Town with her grandmother. They drove home in their new acquisition, a shiny blue Toyota, in a happy mood and quite unable to believe how well everything had turned out thanks to their wonderful neighbour, Jasper Rousseau.

'I can't believe how fortunate we are,' Mrs Smit remarked happily. 'The good Lord has sorted it all out.'

In a few short weeks Jasper had

cleared up the mess from the fire and employed a building contractor to erect another house a short distance away from where the cottage had once stood. Her grandparents had been consulted throughout the process and it was now almost completed; a much larger home with three bedrooms and a kitchen, the like of which Mrs Smit had never seen.

The shining new cooker was her pride and joy, not to mention the granite work surfaces and state-of-the-art refrigerator. She would be able to make her jams in much greater comfort as there was even a convenient ante-room in which to prepare the berries and store the bottles.

The crowning glory, however, was the small roadside shop being built beside the entrance to the farm, just yards from the gateposts. In it they would be able to sell her jams and relishes to the tourists, as well as any fresh fruit in season. There may even be a market for some of the home knitted sweaters she was so skilled at producing.

Johannes would be over the moon at having to manage things; he'd always fancied himself as a shop keeper and there would be more than enough to occupy his days.

Lexi and her grandmother went home to the flat to complete the packing up, happy in the knowledge that Mister Smit had almost completely finished his redesigning of the proposed orchard. It would be even more splendid than before, with better strains of fruit and extra labour for the terraces, supplied, of course, by Jasper. As soon as they had moved into their new home, work would begin on the orchard.

It was an even happier day when they hung up their new curtains and arranged their new furniture. Jasper had refused to take back the cheque he'd given them, leaving enough money to buy the Toyota. They had also acquired various other items her grandmother had always wanted but had never been able to afford. In addition there would also be that extra money from the sale of The Old Brown Teapot.

Lexi was singing softly to herself as she washed the dainty new crockery which her grandmother had chosen with an eye to inviting their neighbour over for dinner.

'The dear boy is eager to sample Lexi's roast lamb and baked apple tart,' Mrs Smit had confided to her husband. And she, Marta Smit, was determined not to let the side down with dishes which were not suitable.

A knock on the kitchen door caused Lexi to glance up in surprise.

'Oh, it's you! Come in, Robbie, it's lovely to see you.'

The child came shyly into the room, holding out a bunch of flowers — white roses and purple lavender picked, she surmised, from the vineyard where each row of vines ended with a white rose bush. Lavender bushes lined the path to the house, and both types of flower had been specifically planted there 'to keep the bees away from the vines', she'd been told.

Robbie thrust the bouquet into her hands. 'These are for you, Miss Smit.' In almost the same breath he asked, 'Do you keep any chocolate chip cookies in your new kitchen?'

'It's called cupboard love,' Jasper's deep voice observed from behind.

Lexi laughed, a carefree sound so that Mrs Smit, bustling into the kitchen, thought how wonderful it was to see that her granddaughter was her usual happy self again.

'Tea and cookies it is,'' the old lady told them with a smile. 'Do come into the living room, my dears. Lexi, put the kettle on.'

It was just as they were about to leave that Robbie astounded the company with his fervently uttered request. Quite unabashed, he looked earnestly into Lexi's startled eyes and begged, 'Will you marry us, Miss Smit? You could come and live at our house and we wouldn't have to eat any more of Mrs Kama's stews.'

In the astonished silence which

followed Jasper's swiftly indrawn breath was rivalled only by Lexi's gasp. How on earth had Robbie known that he was planning to ask the old man for Lexi's hand that very evening? An old fashioned gesture but a very necessary one.

Mister and Mrs Smit exchanged significant looks, for they had already discussed this very possibility in the privacy of their bedroom.

Unaware of the sensation he'd caused, Robbie plunged determinedly on. 'My Papa,' he added just as though it explained everything quite satisfactorily, 'loves your hair and I love your cookies.' With anxious eyes glued to Lexi's face, he waited expectantly for her reply.

Lexi's tinkle of laughter broke the tension, with everyone looking at one another in amusement. Only Jasper's eyes remained intent upon her suddenly glowing face.

'In that case, Robbie,' she declared, 'You'd better start calling me Mama.

But hadn't we better ask your Papa if he approves? I mean, he might not want to stop eating Mrs Kama's stews . . . '

A light came on behind Jasper's eyes. 'Oh, I imagine Robbie's Papa would be more than willing to forego any further mediocre dinners, not to mention inedible desserts . . . providing Lexi is agreeable to baking a constant supply of chocolate chip cookies, that is. But hadn't we better do the thing properly?'

He turned to Mister Smit, who was smiling hugely. 'May I have your granddaughter's hand in marriage, sir?' His deep voice turned gruff. 'It would be my privilege to love her until I die and I intend to endow her with all my worldly goods — small things like an occasional bunch of grapes and the odd bottle of wine.' He added with a grin, 'Naturally there would also be boxes of chocolates and bouquets of flowers from time to time.'

Mister Smit, in order to cover his emotion, replied with a growl, 'You have my every blessing.' Jasper was a man of considerable means and his beloved granddaughter would never again want for anything.

'I notice that the person I am about to marry has not actually asked me yet,' Lexi pointed out in a cross voice which hid the pleasant tingle of excitement that feathered her spine and placed a sparkle in her blue eyes. 'I would also like a say in the matter, for pity's sake.'

Jasper's firm mouth twitched. 'My mistake.'

He folded Lexi in his arms and kissed her soundly, then to Mrs Smit's delight quoted unexpectedly from Solomon's Song. 'Who can find a virtuous woman? Her price is far above rubies . . . '

He lifted his head and looked into her eyes. 'Alexandra Mary Smit, will you marry me? In you I have found a pearl of great price and I love you to distraction, cookies notwithstanding.'

Lexi, who cared neither for pearls nor rubies, had her heart set on something else and told him so. 'You see, Jasper,' she said earnestly, 'Sapphires go very nicely with my blue eyes.'

Jasper's eyes glimmered with tender amusement. 'You shall have whatever your heart desires,' he told her, and kissed her again. 'Only say you will marry me, Lexi. You haven't said yes, yet.'

Lexi's blue eyes rounded in mock surprise. 'Of course I'll marry you, Jasper. And you too, Robbie.'

Jasper closed his own eyes and drew a deep, satisfied breath. He had at long last found his heart's treasure. Robbie would have a steady supply of his heart's desire, too; those chocolate chip cookies would soon be coming out of his adorable ears.

★ ★ ★

February ushered itself out in a blaze of summer heat. Just before the start of the grape harvest Jasper Charles Rousseau and Alexandra Mary Smit were married in the large, whitewashed church in Franschhoek where the bride, radiant in white lace and mountains of tulle, proudly flashed her sapphires. They did indeed go well with her eyes and Gina and Chantal looked positively envious.

After the ceremony the guests returned to Maison Rousseau for the wedding breakfast, where a triumphant Mrs Kama fluttered about like an important butterfly, resplendent in her new purple and yellow outfit with matching head-dress. She hindered the caterers at every turn and ordered poor Gerda about to her heart's content. She was, after all the housekeeper of a very large establishment.

'Did I not tell you, Gerda, that the cross lady in the blue van would make an excellent wife for the master?' she demanded happily as they tucked into Mrs Smit's splendid wedding cake together.

'Yes, Mrs Kama, you did,' Gerda agreed dutifully.

There would be plenty of babies, too, Mrs Kama informed her as an after-thought; she felt it in her bones and she was seldom wrong about these things. There would be six strong boys like the master and four girls with yellow hair like the mistress.

As for young master Robbie, he would have no more bad dreams; he'd be too busy eating the mistress's cookies. What's more, he would grow up to be a fine man just like his father. But best of all was the fact that she, Maria Kama, wife of Jakob the head gardener, excellent housekeeper and cook, would not have to make any more of that awful European food.

In the morning, she resolved happily as she reached for another slice of cake, she would go into town and buy a large bag of corn meal and some of her husband's favourite dried beans. She would cook them to perfection and in the evening they would have their own feast in honour of the occasion.

She'd heard that there were many bargains to be had at that new supermarket in Stellenbosch; the one near the shop with the picture of the brown teapot. They also sold his favourite beer there.

She must certainly remember to tell Jakob . . .

THE END

We do hope that you have enjoyed reading this large print book.

Did you know that all of our titles are available for purchase?

We publish a wide range of high quality large print books including:
Romances, Mysteries, Classics
General Fiction
Non Fiction and Westerns

Special interest titles available in large print are:
The Little Oxford Dictionary
Music Book, Song Book
Hymn Book, Service Book

Also available from us courtesy of Oxford University Press:
Young Readers' Dictionary
(large print edition)
Young Readers' Thesaurus
(large print edition)

For further information or a free brochure, please contact us at:
Ulverscroft Large Print Books Ltd.,
The Green, Bradgate Road, Anstey,
Leicester, LE7 7FU, England.
Tel: (00 44) **0116 236 4325**
Fax: (00 44) **0116 234 0205**

SPECIAL MESSAGE TO READERS

This book is published under the auspices of

THE ULVERSCROFT FOUNDATION

(registered charity No. 264873 UK)

Established in 1972 to provide funds for research, diagnosis and treatment of eye diseases. Examples of contributions made are: —

A Children's Assessment Unit at Moorfield's Hospital, London.

•

Twin operating theatres at the Western Ophthalmic Hospital, London.

•

A Chair of Ophthalmology at the Royal Australian College of Ophthalmologists.

•

The Ulverscroft Children's Eye Unit at the Great Ormond Street Hospital For Sick Children, London.

You can help further the work of the Foundation by making a donation or leaving a legacy. Every contribution, no matter how small, is received with gratitude. Please write for details to:

THE ULVERSCROFT FOUNDATION,
**The Green, Bradgate Road, Anstey,
Leicester LE7 7FU, England.
Telephone: (0116) 236 4325**

In Australia write to:
THE ULVERSCROFT FOUNDATION,
**c/o The Royal Australian and New Zealand
College of Ophthalmologists,
94-98 Chalmers Street, Surry Hills,
N.S.W. 2010, Australia**

A = ?

C 02 0329768